Henry Wadsworth Longfellow

Ballads, Lyrics and Sonnets

From the Poetic Works of Henry Wadsworth Longfellow

Henry Wadsworth Longfellow

Ballads, Lyrics and Sonnets
From the Poetic Works of Henry Wadsworth Longfellow

ISBN/EAN: 9783744782647

Printed in Europe, USA, Canada, Australia, Japan

Cover: Foto ©Andreas Hilbeck / pixelio.de

More available books at **www.hansebooks.com**

LLADS, LYRICS AND SONNETS
FROM THE POETIC WORKS OF
HENRY WADSWORTH
LONGFELLOW

BOSTON AND NEW YORK
HOUGHTON, MIFFLIN AND COMPANY
The Riverside Press, Cambridge
M DCCC LXXXIX

THE ARROW AND THE SONG.

I shot an arrow into the air,
It fell to earth, I knew not where ;
For, so swiftly it flew, the sight
Could not follow it in its flight.

I breathed a song into the air,
It fell to earth, I knew not where ;
For who has sight so keen and strong
That it can follow the flight of song ?

Long, long afterward, in an oak
I found the arrow, still unbroke ;
And the song, from beginning to end,
I found again in the heart of a friend.

CONTENTS

BALLADS AND LYRICS

Contents   *vii*

BALLADS AND LYRICS.

THE SKELETON IN ARMOR.

"SPEAK! speak! thou fearful
  guest!
 Who, with thy hollow breast
Still in rude armor drest,
 Comest to daunt me!
Wrapt not in Eastern balms,
But with thy fleshless palms
Stretched, as if asking alms,
 Why dost thou haunt me?"

Then, from those cavernous eyes
Pale flashes seemed to rise,
As when the Northern skies
 Gleam in December;
And, like the water's flow
Under December's snow,
Came a dull voice of woe
 From the heart's chamber.

" I was a Viking old !
My deeds, though manifold,
No Skald in song has told,
    No Saga taught thee !
Take heed, that in thy verse
Thou dost the tale rehearse,
Else dread a dead man's curse ;
    For this I sought thee.

" Far in the Northern Land,
By the wild Baltic's strand,
I, with my childish hand,
    Tamed the gerfalcon ;
And, with my skates fast-bound,
Skimmed the half-frozen Sound,
That the poor whimpering hound
    Trembled to walk on.

" Oft to his frozen lair
Tracked I the grisly bear,
While from my path the hare
    Fled like a shadow ;
Oft through the forest dark
Followed the were-wolf's bark,
Until the soaring lark
    Sang from the meadow.

" But when I older grew,
  Joining a corsair's crew,
  O'er the dark sea I flew
    With the marauders.
  Wild was the life we led ;
  Many the souls that sped,
  Many the hearts that bled,
    By our stern orders.

" Many a wassail-bout
  Wore the long Winter out ;
  Often our midnight shout
    Set the cocks crowing,
  As we the Berserk's tale
  Measured in cups of ale,
  Draining the oaken pail,
    Filled to o'erflowing.

" Once as I told in glee
  Tales of the stormy sea,
  Soft eyes did gaze on me,
    Burning yet tender ;
  And as the white stars shine
  On the dark Norway pine,
  On that dark heart of mine
    Fell their soft splendor.

" I wooed the blue-eyed maid,
　Yielding, yet half afraid,
　And in the forest's shade
　　Our vows were plighted.
　Under its loosened vest
　Fluttered her little breast,
　Like birds within their nest
　　By the hawk frighted.

" Bright in her father's hall
　Shields gleamed upon the wall,
　Loud sang the minstrels all,
　　Chanting his glory;
　When of old Hildebrand
　I asked his daughter's hand,
　Mute did the minstrels stand
　　To hear my story.

" While the brown ale he quaffed,
　Loud then the champion laughed,
　And as the wind-gusts waft
　　The sea-foam brightly,
　So the loud laugh of scorn,
　Out of those lips unshorn,
　From the deep drinking-horn
　　Blew the foam lightly.

" She was a Prince's child,
  I but a Viking wild,
  And though she blushed and smiled,
    I was discarded !
  Should not the dove so white
  Follow the sea-mew's flight,
  Why did they leave that night
    Her nest unguarded ?

" Scarce had I put to sea,
  Bearing the maid with me,
  Fairest of all was she
    Among the Norsemen !
  When on the white sea-strand,
  Waving his armed hand,
  Saw we old Hildebrand,
    With twenty horsemen.

" Then launched they to the blast,
  Bent like a reed each mast,
  Yet we were gaining fast,
    When the wind failed us ;
  And with a sudden flaw
  Came round the gusty Skaw,
  So that our foe we saw
    Laugh as he hailed us.

" And as to catch the gale
   Round veered the flapping sail,
' Death ! ' was the helmsman's hail,
   ' Death without quarter ! '
Mid-ships with iron keel
Struck we her ribs of steel ;
Down her black hulk did reel
   Through the black water !

" As with his wings aslant,
   Sails the fierce cormorant,
Seeking some rocky haunt,
   With his prey laden, —
So toward the open main,
Beating to sea again,
Through the wild hurricane,
   Bore I the maiden.

" Three weeks we westward bore,
   And when the storm was o'er,
Cloud-like we saw the shore
   Stretching to leeward ;
There for my lady's bower
Built I the lofty tower,
Which, to this very hour,
   Stands looking seaward.

"There lived we many years ;
  Time dried the maiden's tears ;
  She had forgot her fears,
    She was a mother ;
  Death closed her mild blue eyes,
  Under that tower she lies ;
  Ne'er shall the sun arise
    On such another !

"Still grew my bosom then,
  Still as a stagnant fen !
  Hateful to me were men,
    The sunlight hateful !
  In the vast forest here,
  Clad in my warlike gear,
  Fell I upon my spear,
    Oh, death was grateful !

"Thus, seamed with many scars,
  Bursting these prison bars,
  Up to its native stars
    My soul ascended !
  There from the flowing bowl
  Deep drinks the warrior's soul,
  Skoal ! to the Northland ! *skoal !*"
    Thus the tale ended.

THE WRECK OF THE HESPERUS.

T was the schooner Hesperus
    That sailed the wintry sea ;
And the skipper had taken his
    little daughtèr,
    To bear him company.

Blue were her eyes as the fairy-flax,
    Her cheeks like the dawn of day,
And her bosom white as the hawthorn
    buds,
    That ope in the month of May.

The skipper he stood beside the helm,
    His pipe was in his mouth,
And he watched how the veering flaw did
    blow
    The smoke now West, now South.

Then up and spake an old Sailòr,
    Had sailed to the Spanish Main,
" I pray thee, put into yonder port,
    For I fear a hurricane.

"Last night, the moon had a golden ring,
    And to-night no moon we see ! "

The skipper, he blew a whiff from his
   pipe,
   And a scornful laugh laughed he.

Colder and louder blew the wind,
   A gale from the Northeast,
The snow fell hissing in the brine,
   And the billows frothed like yeast.

Down came the storm, and smote amain
   The vessel in its strength ;
She shuddered and paused, like a frighted
   steed,
   Then leaped her cable's length.

"Come hither ! come hither ! my little
   daughtèr,
   And do not tremble so ;
For I can weather the roughest gale
   That ever wind did blow."

He wrapped her warm in his seaman's
   coat
   Against the stinging blast ;
He cut a rope from a broken spar,
   And bound her to the mast.

"O father ! I hear the church-bells ring,
    Oh say, what may it be ? "
" 'T is a fog-bell on a rock-bound
        coast ! " —
    And he steered for the open sea.

"O father ! I hear the sound of guns,
    Oh say, what may it be ? "
" Some ship in distress, that cannot live
    In such an angry sea ! "

"O father ! I see a gleaming light,
    Oh say, what may it be ? "
But the father answered never a word,
    A frozen corpse was he.

Lashed to the helm, all stiff and stark,
    With his face turned to the skies,
The lantern gleamed through the gleam-
        ing snow
    On his fixed and glassy eyes.

Then the maiden clasped her hands and
        prayed
    That savèd she might be ;
And she thought of Christ, who stilled the
        wave,
    On the Lake of Galilee.

And fast through the midnight dark and
    drear,
    Through the whistling sleet and
    snow,
Like a sheeted ghost, the vessel swept
    Tow'rds the reef of Norman's Woe.

And ever the fitful gusts between
    A sound came from the land ;
It was the sound of the trampling surf
    On the rocks and the hard sea-sand.

The breakers were right beneath her
    bows,
    She drifted a dreary wreck,
And a whooping billow swept the crew
    Like icicles from her deck.

She struck where the white and fleecy
    waves
    Looked soft as carded wool,
But the cruel rocks, they gored her side
    Like the horns of an angry bull.

Her rattling shrouds, all sheathed in ice,
    With the masts went by the board ;
Like a vessel of glass, she stove and sank,
    Ho ! ho ! the breakers roared.

At daybreak, on the bleak sea-beach,
    A fisherman stood aghast,
To see the form of a maiden fair
    Lashed close to a drifting mast.

The salt sea was frozen on her breast,
    The salt tears in her eyes;
And he saw her hair, like the brown sea-
      weed,
    On the billows fall and rise.

Such was the wreck of the Hesperus,
    In the midnight and the snow!
Christ save us all from a death like this,
    On the reef of Norman's Woe!

KING CHRISTIAN.

A NATIONAL SONG OF DENMARK.

KING CHRISTIAN stood by the
    lofty mast
      In mist and smoke;
His sword was hammering so fast,
Through Gothic helm and brain it passed;
Then sank each hostile hulk and mast,
    In mist and smoke.

" Fly ! " shouted they, " fly, he who can !
Who braves of Denmark's Christian
    The stroke ? "

Nils Juel gave heed to the tempest's roar,
    Now is the hour !
He hoisted his blood-red flag once more,
And smote upon the foe full sore,
And shouted loud, through the tempest's
    roar,
    " Now is the hour ! "
" Fly ! " shouted they, " for shelter fly !
Of Denmark's Juel who can defy
    The power ? "

North Sea ! a glimpse of Wessel rent
    Thy murky sky !
Then champions to thine arms were sent;
Terror and Death glared where he went ;
From the waves was heard a wail, that
    rent
    Thy murky sky !
From Denmark thunders Tordenskiol',
Let each to Heaven commend his soul,
    And fly !

Path of the Dane to fame and might !
    Dark-rolling wave !

Receive thy friend, who, scorning flight,
Goes to meet danger with despite,
Proudly as thou the tempest's might,
    Dark-rolling wave !
And amid pleasures and alarms,
And war and victory, be thine arms
    My grave !

BEWARE!

[A GERMAN VOLKSLIED.]

 KNOW a maiden fair to see,
    Take care !
She can both false and friendly
    be,
    Beware ! Beware !
    Trust her not,
She is fooling thee !

She has two eyes, so soft and brown,
    Take care !
She gives a side-glance and looks down,
    Beware ! Beware !
    Trust her not,
She is fooling thee !

And she has hair of a golden hue,
    Take care !
And what she says, it is not true,
    Beware !   Beware !
    Trust her not,
She is fooling thee !

She has a bosom as white as snow,
    Take care !
She knows how much it is best to show,
    Beware !   Beware !
    Trust her not,
She is fooling thee !

She gives thee a garland woven fair,
    Take care !
It is a fool's-cap for thee to wear,
    Beware !   Beware !
    Trust her not,
She is fooling thee !

THE CASTLE BY THE SEA.

[FROM THE GERMAN OF UHLAND.]

" HAST thou seen that lordly cas-
    tle,
    That Castle by the Sea ?

Golden and red above it
    The clouds float gorgeously.

"And fain it would stoop downward
    To the mirrored wave below;
And fain it would soar upward
    In the evening's crimson glow."

"Well have I seen that castle,
    That Castle by the Sea,
And the moon above it standing,
    And the mist rise solemnly."

"The winds and the waves of ocean,
    Had they a merry chime?
Didst thou hear, from those lofty cham-
        bers,
    The harp and the minstrel's rhyme?"

"The winds and the waves of ocean,
    They rested quietly,
But I heard on the gale a sound of wail,
    And tears came to mine eye."

"And sawest thou on the turrets
    The King and his royal bride?
And the wave of their crimson mantles?
    And the golden crown of pride?

" Led they not forth, in rapture,
  A beauteous maiden there ?
Resplendent as the morning sun,
  Beaming with golden hair ? "

" Well saw I the ancient parents,
  Without the crown of pride ;
They were moving slow, in weeds of
    woe,
  No maiden was by their side ! "

THE VILLAGE BLACKSMITH.

UNDER a spreading chestnut-tree
    The village smithy stands ;
  The smith, a mighty man is he,
    With large and sinewy hands ;
And the muscles of his brawny arms
  Are strong as iron bands.

His hair is crisp, and black, and long,
  His face is like the tan ;
His brow is wet with honest sweat,
  He earns whate'er he can,

And looks the whole world in the face,
　For he owes not any man.

Week in, week out, from morn till night,
　You can hear his bellows blow ;
You can hear him swing his heavy sledge,
　With measured beat and slow,
Like a sexton ringing the village bell,
　When the evening sun is low.

And children coming home from school
　Look in at the open door ;
They love to see the flaming forge,
　And hear the bellows roar,
And catch the burning sparks that fly
　Like chaff from a threshing-floor.

He goes on Sunday to the church,
　And sits among his boys ;
He hears the parson pray and preach,
　He hears his daughter's voice,
Singing in the village choir,
　And it makes his heart rejoice.

It sounds to him like her mother's voice,
　Singing in Paradise !

He needs must think of her once more,
How in the grave she lies;
And with his hard, rough hand he wipes
A tear out of his eyes.

Toiling, — rejoicing, — sorrowing,
Onward through life he goes;
Each morning sees some task begin,
Each evening sees it close;
Something attempted, something done,
Has earned a night's repose.

Thanks, thanks to thee, my worthy friend,
For the lesson thou hast taught!
Thus at the flaming forge of life
Our fortunes must be wrought;
Thus on its sounding anvil shaped
Each burning deed and thought.

THE RAINY DAY.

HE day is cold, and dark, and
dreary;
It rains, and the wind is never
weary;

The vine still clings to the mouldering
    wall,
But at every gust the dead leaves fall,
    And the day is dark and dreary.

My life is cold, and dark, and dreary;
It rains, and the wind is never weary;
My thoughts still cling to the mouldering
        Past,
But the hopes of youth fall thick in the
        blast,
    And the days are dark and dreary.

Be still, sad heart! and cease repining;
Behind the clouds is the sun still shining;
Thy fate is the common fate of all,
Into each life some rain must fall,
    Some days must be dark and dreary.

TO THE RIVER CHARLES.

IVER ! that in silence windest
        Through the meadows, bright
            and free,
Till at length thy rest thou findest
    In the bosom of the sea !

Four long years of mingled feeling,
  Half in rest, and half in strife,
I have seen thy waters stealing
  Onward, like the stream of life.

Thou hast taught me, Silent River!
  Many a lesson, deep and long;
Thou hast been a generous giver;
  I can give thee but a song.

Oft in sadness and in illness,
  I have watched thy current glide,
Till the beauty of its stillness
  Overflowed me, like a tide.

And in better hours and brighter,
  When I saw thy waters gleam,
I have felt my heart beat lighter,
  And leap onward with thy stream.

Not for this alone I love thee,
  Nor because thy waves of blue
From celestial seas above thee
  Take their own celestial hue.

Where yon shadowy woodlands hide thee.
  And thy waters disappear,

Friends I love have dwelt beside thee,
   And have made thy margin dear.

More than this ; — thy name reminds me
   Of three friends, all true and tried ;
And that name, like magic, binds me
   Closer, closer to thy side.

Friends my soul with joy remembers !
   How like quivering flames they start,
When I fan the living embers
   On the hearth-stone of my heart !

'T is for this, thou Silent River !
   That my spirit leans to thee ;
Thou hast been a generous giver,
   Take this idle song from me.

ANNIE OF THARAW.

[FROM THE LOW GERMAN OF SIMON DACH.]

ANNIE OF THARAW, my true
     love of old,
     She is my life, and my goods,
     and my gold.

Annie of Tharaw, her heart once again
To me has surrendered in joy and in
    pain.

Annie of Tharaw, my riches, my good,
Thou, O my soul, my flesh, and my blood!

Then come the wild weather, come sleet
    or come snow,
We will stand by each other, however it
    blow.

Oppression, and sickness, and sorrow, and
    pain
Shall be to our true love as links to the
    chain.

As the palm-tree standeth so straight and
    so tall,
The more the hail beats, and the more the
    rains fall, —

So love in our hearts shall grow mighty
    and strong,
Through crosses, through sorrows, through
    manifold wrong.

Shouldst thou be torn from me to wander
    alone
In a desolate land where the sun is scarce
    known, —

Through forests I 'll follow, and where
    the sea flows,
Through ice, and through iron, through
    armies of foes.

Annie of Tharaw, my light and my sun,
The threads of our two lives are woven in
    one.

Whate'er I have bidden thee thou hast
    obeyed,
Whatever forbidden thou hast not gain-
    said.

How in the turmoil of life can love stand,
Where there is not one heart, and one
    mouth, and one hand ?

Some seek for dissension, and trouble,
    and strife ;
Like a dog and a cat live such man and
    wife.

Annie of Tharaw, such is not our love ;
Thou art my lambkin, my chick, and my
dove.

Whate'er my desire is, in thine may be
seen ;
I am king of the household, and thou art
its queen.

It is this, O my Annie, my heart's sweetest
rest,
That makes of us twain but one soul in
one breast.

This turns to a heaven the hut where we
dwell ;
While wrangling soon changes a home to
a hell.

MAIDENHOOD.

MAIDEN ! with the meek, brown
eyes,
In whose orbs a shadow lies
Like the dusk in evening skies !

Thou whose locks outshine the sun,
Golden tresses, wreathed in one,
As the braided streamlets run !

Standing, with reluctant feet,
Where the brook and river meet,
Womanhood and childhood fleet !

Gazing, with a timid glance,
On the brooklet's swift advance,
On the river's broad expanse !

Deep and still, that gliding stream
Beautiful to thee must seem,
As the river of a dream.

Then why pause with indecision,
When bright angels in thy vision
Beckon thee to fields Elysian ?

Seest thou shadows sailing by,
As the dove, with startled eye,
Sees the falcon's shadow fly ?

Hearest thou voices on the shore,
That our ears perceive no more,
Deafened by the cataract's roar ?

Oh, thou child of many prayers!
Life hath quicksands, Life hath snares!
Care and age come unawares!

Like the swell of some sweet tune,
Morning rises into noon,
May glides onward into June.

Childhood is the bough, where slumbered
Birds and blossoms many-numbered;—
Age, that bough with snows encumbered.

Gather, then, each flower that grows,
When the young heart overflows,
To embalm that tent of snows.

Bear a lily in thy hand;
Gates of brass cannot withstand
One touch of that magic wand.

Bear through sorrow, wrong, and ruth,
In thy heart the dew of youth,
On thy lips the smile of truth.

Oh, that dew, like balm, shall steal
Into wounds that cannot heal,
Even as sleep our eyes doth seal;

And that smile, like sunshine, dart
Into many a sunless heart,
For a smile of God thou art.

EXCELSIOR.

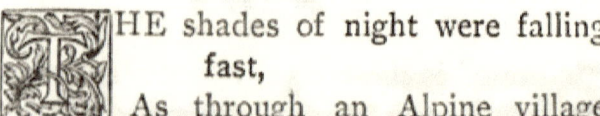

THE shades of night were falling
    fast,
As through an Alpine village
    passed
A youth, who bore, 'mid snow and ice,
A banner with the strange device,
        Excelsior!

His brow was sad ; his eye beneath
Flashed like a falchion from its sheath,
And like a silver clarion rung
The accents of that unknown tongue,
        Excelsior !

In happy homes he saw the light
Of household fires gleam warm and
    bright ;
Above, the spectral glaciers shone,
And from his lips escaped a groan,
        Excelsior !

"Try not the Pass !" the old man said;
" Dark lowers the tempest overhead,
The roaring torrent is deep and wide !"
And loud that clarion voice replied,
Excelsior !

"Oh stay," the maiden said, " and rest
Thy weary head upon this breast !"
A tear stood in his bright blue eye,
But still he answered, with a sigh,
Excelsior !

" Beware the pine-tree's withered branch !
Beware the awful avalanche !"
This was the peasant's last Good-night,
A voice replied, far up the height,
Excelsior !

At break of day, as heavenward
The pious monks of Saint Bernard
Uttered the oft-repeated prayer,
A voice cried through the startled air,
Excelsior !

A traveller, by the faithful hound,
Half-buried in the snow was found,
Still grasping in his hand of ice

That banner with the strange device,
>   Excelsior !

There in the twilight cold and gray,
Lifeless, but beautiful, he lay,
And from the sky, serene and far,
A voice fell, like a falling star,
>   Excelsior !

THE WARNING.

EWARE ! The Israelite of old,
>   who tore
> The lion in his path, — when,
>   poor and blind,

He saw the blessed light of heaven no
>   more,
> Shorn of his noble strength and forced
>   to grind
In prison, and at last led forth to be
A pander to Philistine revelry, —

Upon the pillars of the temple laid
>   His desperate hands, and in its over-
>   throw

Destroyed himself, and with him those
  who made
A cruel mockery of his sightless woe;
The poor, blind Slave, the scoff and jest
  of all,
Expired, and thousands perished in the
  fall!

There is a poor, blind Samson in this
  land,
  Shorn of his strength and bound in
    bonds of steel,
Who may, in some grim revel, raise his
  hand,
  And shake the pillars of this Common-
    weal,
Till the vast Temple of our liberties
A shapeless mass of wreck and rubbish
  lies.

THE BELFRY OF BRUGES.

CARILLON.

N the ancient town of Bruges,
  In the quaint old Flemish city,
    As the evening shades descended,

Low and loud and sweetly blended,
Low at times and loud at times,
And changing like a poet's rhymes,
Rang the beautiful wild chimes
From the Belfry in the market
Of the ancient town of Bruges.

Then, with deep sonorous clangor
Calmly answering their sweet anger,
When the wrangling bells had ended,
Slowly struck the clock eleven,
And, from out the silent heaven,
Silence on the town descended.
Silence, silence everywhere,
On the earth and in the air,
Save that footsteps here and there
Of some burgher home returning,
By the street lamps faintly burning,
For a moment woke the echoes
Of the ancient town of Bruges.

But amid my broken slumbers
Still I heard those magic numbers,
As they loud proclaimed the flight
And stolen marches of the night ;
Till their chimes in sweet collision
Mingled with each wandering vision,

Mingled with the fortune-telling
Gypsy-bands of dreams and fancies,
Which amid the waste expanses
Of the silent land of trances
Have their solitary dwelling;
All else seemed asleep in Bruges,
In the quaint old Flemish city.

And I thought how like these chimes
Are the poet's airy rhymes,
All his rhymes and roundelays,
His conceits, and songs, and ditties,
From the belfry of his brain,
Scattered downward, though in vain,
On the roofs and stones of cities!
For by night the drowsy ear
Under its curtains cannot hear,
And by day men go their ways,
Hearing the music as they pass,
But deeming it no more, alas!
Than the hollow sound of brass.

Yet perchance a sleepless wight,
Lodging at some humble inn
In the narrow lanes of life,
When the dusk and hush of night
Shut out the incessant din

Of daylight and its toil and strife,
May listen with a calm delight
To the poet's melodies,
Till he hears, or dreams he hears,
Intermingled with the song,
Thoughts that he has cherished long;
Hears amid the chime and singing
The bells of his own village ringing,
And wakes, and finds his slumberous
    eyes
Wet with most delicious tears.

Thus dreamed I, as by night I lay
In Bruges, at the Fleur-de-Blé,
Listening with a wild delight
To the chimes that, through the night,
Rang their changes from the Belfry
Of that quaint old Flemish city.

In the market-place of Bruges stands
    the belfry old and brown;
Thrice consumed and thrice rebuilded,
    still it watches o'er the town.

As the summer morn was breaking, on
    that lofty tower I stood,
And the world threw off the darkness, like
    the weeds of widowhood.

Thick with towns and hamlets studded,
    and with streams and vapors gray,
Like a shield embossed with silver, round
    and vast the landscape lay.

At my feet the city slumbered.   From its
    chimneys, here and there,
Wreaths of snow-white smoke, ascending,
    vanished, ghost-like, into air.

Not a sound rose from the city at that
    early morning hour,
But I heard a heart of iron beating in the
    ancient tower.

From their nests beneath the rafters sang
    the swallows wild and high ;
And the world, beneath me sleeping,
    seemed more distant than the sky.

Then most musical and solemn, bringing
    back the olden times,

With their strange, unearthly changes
    rang the melancholy chimes,

Like the psalms from some old cloister,
    when the nuns sing in the choir;
And the great bell tolled among them, like
    the chanting of a friar.

Visions of the days departed, shadowy
    phantoms filled my brain;
They who live in history only seemed to
    walk the earth again;

All the Foresters of Flanders, — mighty
    Baldwin Bras de Fer,
Lyderick du Bucq and Cressy, Philip, Guy
    de Dampierre.

I beheld the pageants splendid that
    adorned those days of old;
Stately dames, like queens attended,
    knights who bore the Fleece of
    Gold;

Lombard and Venetian merchants with
    deep-laden argosies;
Ministers from twenty nations; more than
    royal pomp and ease.

I beheld proud Maximilian, kneeling hum-
    bly on the ground;
I beheld the gentle Mary, hunting with
    her hawk and hound;

And her lighted bridal-chamber, where a
    duke slept with the queen,
And the armed guard around them, and
    the sword unsheathed between.

I beheld the Flemish weavers, with Na-
    mur and Juliers bold,
Marching homeward from the bloody bat-
    tle of the Spurs of Gold;

Saw the fight at Minnewater, saw the
    White Hoods moving west,
Saw great Artevelde victorious scale the
    Golden Dragon's nest.

And again the whiskered Spaniard all the
    land with terror smote;
And again the wild alarum sounded from
    the tocsin's throat;

Till the bell of Ghent responded o'er
    lagoon and dike of sand,

"I am Roland! I am Roland! there is
    victory in the land!"

Then the sound of drums aroused me.
    The awakened city's roar
Chased the phantoms I had summoned
    back into their graves once more.

Hours had passed away like minutes; and,
    before I was aware,
Lo! the shadow of the belfry crossed the
    sun-illumined square.

A GLEAM OF SUNSHINE.

THIS is the place.   Stand still, my
    steed,
    Let me review the scene,
And summon from the shadowy Past
    The forms that once have been.

The Past and Present here unite
    Beneath Time's flowing tide,
Like footprints hidden by a brook,
    But seen on either side.

Here runs the highway to the town ;
  There the green lane descends,
Through which I walked to church with
      thee,
  O gentlest of my friends !

The shadow of the linden-trees
  Lay moving on the grass ;
Between them and the moving boughs,
  A shadow, thou didst pass.

Thy dress was like the lilies,
  And thy heart as pure as they :
One of God's holy messengers
  Did walk with me that day.

I saw the branches of the trees
  Bend down thy touch to meet,
The clover-blossoms in the grass
  Rise up to kiss thy feet.

" Sleep, sleep to-day, tormenting cares,
  Of earth and folly born ! "
Solemnly sang the village choir
  On that sweet Sabbath morn.

Through the closed blinds the golden sun
  Poured in a dusty beam,

Like the celestial ladder seen
   By Jacob in his dream.

And ever and anon, the wind,
   Sweet-scented with the hay,
Turned o'er the hymn-book's fluttering
     leaves
   That on the window lay.

Long was the good man's sermon,
   Yet it seemed not so to me;
For he spake of Ruth the beautiful,
   And still I thought of thee.

Long was the prayer he uttered,
   Yet it seemed not so to me;
For in my heart I prayed with him,
   And still I thought of thee.

But now, alas! the place seems changed;
   Thou art no longer here:
Part of the sunshine of the scene
   With thee did disappear.

Though thoughts, deep-rooted in my heart,
   Like pine-trees dark and high,
Subdue the light of noon, and breathe
   A low and ceaseless sigh;

This memory brightens o'er the past,
   As when the sun, concealed
Behind some cloud that near us hangs
   Shines on a distant field.

TO A CHILD.

DEAR child ! how radiant on thy
      mother's knee,
  With merry-making eyes and
      jocund smiles,
Thou gazest at the painted tiles,
Whose figures grace,
With many a grotesque form and face,
The ancient chimney of thy nursery !
The lady with the gay macaw,
The dancing girl, the grave bashaw
With bearded lip and chin ; '
And, leaning idly o'er his gate,
Beneath the imperial fan of state,
The Chinese mandarin.

With what a look of proud command
Thou shakest in thy little hand
The coral rattle with its silver bells,

Making a merry tune !
Thousands of years in Indian seas
That coral grew, by slow degrees,
Until some deadly and wild monsoon
Dashed it on Coromandel's sand !
Those silver bells
Reposed of yore,
As shapeless ore,
Far down in the deep-sunken wells
Of darksome mines,
In some obscure and sunless place,
Beneath huge Chimborazo's base,
Or Potosi's o'erhanging pines !
And thus for thee, O little child,
Through many a danger and escape,
The tall ships passed the stormy cape ;
For thee in foreign lands remote,
Beneath a burning, tropic clime,
The Indian peasant, chasing the wild goat,
Himself as swift and wild,
In falling, clutched the frail arbute,
The fibres of whose shallow root,
Uplifted from the soil, betrayed
The silver veins beneath it laid,
The buried treasures of the miser, Time.

But, lo ! thy door is left ajar !
Thou hearest footsteps from afar !

And, at the sound,
Thou turnest round
With quick and questioning eyes,
Like one who, in a foreign land,
Beholds on every hand
Some source of wonder and surprise !
And, restlessly, impatiently,
Thou strivest, strugglest, to be free.

The four walls of thy nursery
Are now like prison walls to thee.
No more thy mother's smiles,
No more the painted tiles,
Delight thee, nor the playthings on the
     floor,
That won thy little, beating heart before ;
Thou strugglest for the open door.

Through these once solitary halls
Thy pattering footstep falls.
The sound of thy merry voice
Makes the old walls
Jubilant, and they rejoice
With the joy of thy young heart,
O'er the light of whose gladness
No shadows of sadness
From the sombre background of memory
     start.

Once, ah, once, within these walls,
One whom memory oft recalls,
The Father of his Country, dwelt.
And yonder meadows broad and damp
The fires of the besieging camp
Encircled with a burning belt.
Up and down these echoing stairs,
Heavy with the weight of cares,
Sounded his majestic tread ;
Yes, within this very room
Sat he in those hours of gloom,
Weary both in heart and head.

But what are these grave thoughts to thee ?
Out, out ! into the open air !
Thy only dream is liberty,
Thou carest little how or where.
I see thee eager at thy play,
Now shouting to the apples on the tree,
With cheeks as round and red as they ;
And now among the yellow stalks,
Among the flowering shrubs and plants,
As restless as the bee.
Along the garden walks,
The tracks of thy small carriage-wheels I
          trace ;
And see at every turn how they efface

Whole villages of sand-roofed tents,
That rise like golden domes
Above the cavernous and secret homes
Of wandering and nomadic tribes of ants.
Ah, cruel little Tamerlane,
Who, with thy dreadful reign,
Dost persecute and overwhelm
These hapless Troglodytes of thy realm!

What! tired already! with those sup-
        pliant looks,
And voice more beautiful than a poet's
        books
Or murmuring sound of water as it flows,
Thou comest back to parley with repose!
This rustic seat in the old apple-tree,
With its o'erhanging golden canopy
Of leaves illuminate with autumnal hues,
And shining with the argent light of dews,
Shall for a season be our place of rest.
Beneath us, like an oriole's pendent nest,
From which the laughing birds have taken
        wing,
By thee abandoned, hangs thy vacant
        swing.
Dream-like the waters of the river gleam;
A sailless vessel drops adown the stream,

And like it, to a sea as wide and deep,
Thou driftest gently down the tides of
    sleep.

O child ! O new-born denizen
Of life's great city! on thy head
The glory of the morn is shed,
Like a celestial benison !
Here at the portal thou dost stand,
And with thy little hand
Thou openest the mysterious gate
Into the future's undiscovered land.
I see its valves expand,
As at the touch of Fate !
Into those realms of love and hate,
Into that darkness blank and drear,
By some prophetic feeling taught,
I launch the bold, adventurous thought,
Freighted with hope and fear ;
As upon subterranean streams,
In caverns unexplored and dark,
Men sometimes launch a fragile bark,
Laden with flickering fire,
And watch its swift-receding beams,
Until at length they disappear,
And in the distant dark expire.

By what astrology of fear or hope
Dare I to cast thy horoscope !
Like the new moon thy life appears ;
A little strip of silver light,
And widening outward into night
The shadowy disk of future years ;
And yet upon its outer rim,
A luminous circle, faint and dim,
And scarcely visible to us here,
Rounds and completes the perfect sphere ;
A prophecy and intimation,
A pale and feeble adumbration,
Of the great world of light, that lies
Behind all human destinies.

Ah ! if thy fate, with anguish fraught,
Should be to wet the dusty soil
With the hot tears and sweat of toil, —
To struggle with imperious thought,
Until the overburdened brain,
Weary with labor, faint with pain,
Like a jarred pendulum, retain
Only its motion, not its power, —
Remember, in that perilous hour,
When most afflicted and oppressed,
From labor there shall come forth rest.

And if a more auspicious fate
On thy advancing steps await,
Still let it ever be thy pride
To linger by the laborer's side ;
With words of sympathy or song
To cheer the dreary march along
Of the great army of the poor,
O'er desert sand, o'er dangerous moor.
Nor to thyself the task shall be
Without reward ; for thou shalt learn
The wisdom early to discern
True beauty in utility ;
As great Pythagoras of yore,
Standing beside the blacksmith's door,
And hearing the hammers, as they smote
The anvils with a different note,
Stole from the varying tones, that hung
Vibrant on every iron tongue,
The secret of the sounding wire,
And formed the seven-chorded lyre.

Enough ! I will not play the Seer ;
I will no longer strive to ope
The mystic volume, where appear
The herald Hope, forerunning Fear,
And Fear, the pursuivant of Hope.
Thy destiny remains untold ;

For, like Acestes' shaft of old,
  The swift thought kindles as it flies,
  And burns to ashes in the skies.

THE DAY IS DONE.

THE day is done, and the dark-
    ness
  Falls from the wings of Night,
As a feather is wafted downward
  From an eagle in his flight.

I see the lights of the village
  Gleam through the rain and the mist,
· And a feeling of sadness comes o'er me
  That my soul cannot resist:

A feeling of sadness and longing,
  That is not akin to pain,
And resembles sorrow only
  As the mist resembles the rain.

Come, read to me some poem,
  Some simple and heartfelt lay,
That shall soothe this restless feeling,
  And banish the thoughts of day.

Not from the grand old masters,
　　Not from the bards sublime,
Whose distant footsteps echo
　　Through the corridors of Time.

For, like strains of martial music,
　　Their mighty thoughts suggest
Life's endless toil and endeavor;
　　And to-night I long for rest.

Read from some humbler poet,
　　Whose songs gushed from his heart,
As showers from the clouds of summer,
　　Or tears from the eyelids start;

Who, through long days of labor,
　　And nights devoid of ease,
Still heard in his soul the music
　　Of wonderful melodies.

Such songs have power to quiet
　　The restless pulse of care,
And come like the benediction
　　That follows after prayer.

Then read from the treasured volume
　　The poem of thy choice,

And lend to the rhyme of the poet
  The beauty of thy voice.

And the night shall be filled with music,
  And the cares, that infest the day,
Shall fold their tents, like the Arabs,
  And as silently steal away.

THE OLD CLOCK ON THE STAIRS.

SOMEWHAT back from the vil-
      lage street
    Stands the old-fashioned country
      seat.
Across its antique portico
Tall poplar-trees their shadows throw ;
And from its station in the hall
An ancient timepiece says to all, —
    " Forever — never !
    Never — forever ! "

Half-way up the stairs it stands,
And points and beckons with its hands
From its case of massive oak,
Like a monk, who, under his cloak,
Crosses himself, and sighs, alas !

With sorrowful voice to all who pass, —
 " Forever — never !
  Never — forever ! "

By day its voice is low and light ;
But in the silent dead of night,
Distinct as a passing footstep's fall,
It echoes along the vacant hall,
Along the ceiling, along the floor,
And seems to say, at each chamber-door,
 " Forever — never !
  Never — forever ! "

Through days of sorrow and of mirth,
Through days of death and days of birth,
Through every swift vicissitude
Of changeful time, unchanged it has stood,
And as if, like God, it all things saw,
It calmly repeats those words of awe, —
 " Forever — never !
  Never — forever ! "

In that mansion used to be
Free-hearted Hospitality ;
His great fires up the chimney roared ;
The stranger feasted at his board ;
But, like the skeleton at the feast,

That warning timepiece never ceased, —
    " Forever — never !
      Never — forever ! '

There groups of merry children played,
There youths and maidens dreaming
    strayed ;
O precious hours !   O golden prime,
And affluence of love and time !
Even as a miser counts his gold,
Those hours the ancient timepiece told, —
    " Forever — never !
      Never — forever ! "

From that chamber, clothed in white,
The bride came forth on her wedding
    night ;
There, in that silent room below,
The dead lay in his shroud of snow ;
And in the hush that followed the prayer,
Was heard the old clock on the stair, —
    " Forever — never !
      Never — forever ! "

All are scattered now and fled,
Some are married, some are dead ;
And when I ask, with throbs of pain,

"Ah! when shall they all meet again?"
As in the days long since gone by,
The ancient timepiece makes reply, —
　　" Forever — never!
　　Never — forever!"

Never here, forever there,
Where all parting, pain, and care,
And death, and time shall disappear, —
Forever there, but never here!
The horologe of Eternity
Sayeth this incessantly, —
　　" Forever — never!
　　Never — forever!"

SEAWEED.

WHEN descends on the Atlantic
　　　The gigantic
　　Storm-wind of the equinox,
Landward in his wrath he scourges
　　The toiling surges,
Laden with seaweed from the rocks:

From Bermuda's reefs; from edges
　　Of sunken ledges,

In some far-off, bright Azore ;
From Bahama, and the dashing,
  Silver-flashing
Surges of San Salvador ;

From the tumbling surf, that buries
  The Orkneyan skerries,
Answering the hoarse Hebrides ;
And from wrecks of ships, and drifting
  Spars, uplifting
On the desolate, rainy seas ;—

Ever drifting, drifting, drifting
  On the shifting
Currents of the restless main ;
Till in sheltered coves, and reaches
  Of sandy beaches,
All have found repose again.

So when storms of wild emotion
  Strike the ocean
Of the poet's soul, erelong
From each cave and rocky fastness,
  In its vastness,
Floats some fragment of a song :

From the far-off isles enchanted,
  Heaven has planted

With the golden fruit of Truth ;
From the flashing surf, whose vision
    Gleams Elysian
In the tropic clime of Youth ;

From the strong Will, and the Endeavor
    That forever
Wrestle with the tides of Fate ;
From the wreck of Hopes far-scattered,
    Tempest-shattered,
Floating waste and desolate ; —

Ever drifting, drifting, drifting
    On the shifting
Currents of the restless heart ;
Till at length in books recorded,
    They, like hoarded
Household words, no more depart.

SIR HUMPHREY GILBERT.

OUTHWARD with fleet of ice
    Sailed the corsair Death ;
Wild and **fast** blew the blast,
And the east-wind was his breath.

His lordly ships of ice
   Glisten in the sun ;
On each side, like pennons wide,
   Flashing crystal streamlets run.

His sails of white sea-mist
   Dripped with silver rain ;
But where he passed there were cast
   Leaden shadows o'er the main.

Eastward from Campobello
   Sir Humphrey Gilbert sailed ;
Three days or more seaward he bore,
   Then, alas ! the land-wind failed.

Alas ! the land-wind failed,
   And ice-cold grew the night ;
And nevermore, on sea or shore,
   Should Sir Humphrey see the light.

He sat upon the deck,
   The Book was in his hand ;
" Do not fear ! Heaven is as near,"
   He said, " by water as by land ! "

In the first watch of the night,
   Without a signal's sound,

Out of the sea, mysteriously,
  The fleet of Death rose all around.

The moon and the evening star
  Were hanging in the shrouds;
Every mast, as it passed,
  Seemed to rake the passing clouds.

They grappled with their prize,
  At midnight black and cold!
As of a rock was the shock;
  Heavily the ground-swell rolled.

Southward through day and dark,
  They drift in close embrace,
With mist and rain, o'er the open main;
  Yet there seems no change of place.

Southward, forever southward,
  They drift through dark and day;
And like a dream, in the Gulf-Stream
  Sinking, vanish all away.

THE FIRE OF DRIFT-WOOD.

DEVEREUX FARM, NEAR MARBLEHEAD.

E sat within the farm-house old,
  Whose windows, looking o'er
    the bay,
Gave to the sea-breeze damp and cold,
  An easy entrance, night and day.

Not far away we saw the port,
  The strange, old-fashioned, silent town,
The lighthouse, the dismantled fort,
  The wooden houses, quaint and brown.

We sat and talked until the night,
  Descending, filled the little room ;
Our faces faded from the sight,
  Our voices only broke the gloom.

We spake of many a vanished scene,
  Of what we once had thought and said,
Of what had been, and might have been,
  And who was changed, and who was
    dead ;

And all that fills the hearts of friends,
  When first they feel, with secret pain,

Their lives thenceforth have separate
    ends,
And never can be one again;

The first slight swerving of the heart,
    That words are powerless to express,
And leave it still unsaid in part,
    Or say it in too great excess.

The very tones in which we spake
    Had something strange, I could but
        mark;
The leaves of memory seemed to make
    A mournful rustling in the dark.

Oft died the words upon our lips,
    As suddenly, from out the fire
Built of the wreck of stranded ships,
    The flames would leap and then expire.

And, as their splendor flashed and failed,
    We thought of wrecks upon the main,
Of ships dismasted, that were hailed
    And sent no answer back again.

The windows, rattling in their frames,
    The ocean, roaring up the beach,

The gusty blast, the bickering flames,
  All mingled vaguely in our speech ;

Until they made themselves a part
  Of fancies floating through the brain,
The long-lost ventures of the heart,
  That send no answers back again.

O flames that glowed ! O hearts that
    yearned !
  They were indeed too much akin,
The drift-wood fire without that burned,
  The thoughts that burned and glowed
    within.

❧

RESIGNATION.

THERE is no flock, however
    watched and tended,
  But one dead lamb is there !
There is no fireside, howsoe'er defended,
  But has one vacant chair !

The air is full of farewells to the dying,
  And mournings for the dead ;

The heart of Rachel, for her children
    crying,
  Will not be comforted!

Let us be patient! These severe afflic-
    tions
  Not from the ground arise,
But oftentimes celestial benedictions
  Assume this dark disguise.

We see but dimly through the mists and
    vapors;
  Amid these earthly damps
What seem to us but sad, funereal tapers
  May be heaven's distant lamps.

There is no Death! What seems so is
    transition;
  This life of mortal breath
Is but a suburb of the life elysian,
  Whose portal we call Death.

She is not dead, — the child of our affec-
    tion, —
  But gone unto that school
Where she no longer needs our poor pro-
    tection,
  And Christ himself doth rule.

In that great cloister's stillness and seclu-
      sion,
  By guardian angels led,
Safe from temptation, safe from sin's pol-
      lution,
  She lives, whom we call dead.

Day after day we think what she is doing
  In those bright realms of air ;
Year after year, her tender steps pursuing,
  Behold her grown more fair.

Thus do we walk with her, and keep un-
      broken
  The bond which nature gives,
Thinking that our remembrance, though
      unspoken,
  May reach her where she lives.

Not as a child shall we again behold her ;
  For when with raptures wild
In our embraces we again enfold her,
  She will not be a child ;

But a fair maiden, in her Father's man-
      sion,
  Clothed with celestial grace ;

And beautiful with all the soul's expan-
    sion
Shall we behold her face.

And though at times impetuous with emo-
    tion
And anguish long suppressed,
The swelling heart heaves moaning like
    the ocean,
That cannot be at rest, —

We will be patient, and assuage the feeling
    We may not wholly stay ;
By silence sanctifying, not concealing,
    The grief that must have way.

SAND OF THE DESERT IN AN HOUR-
GLASS.

HANDFUL of red sand, from
    the hot clime
Of Arab deserts brought,
Within this glass becomes the spy of
    Time,
The minister of Thought.

How many weary centuries has it been
    About those deserts blown !
How many strange vicissitudes has seen,
    How many histories known !

Perhaps the camels of the Ishmaelite
    Trampled and passed it o'er,
When into Egypt from the patriarch's
        sight
    His favorite son they bore.

Perhaps the feet of Moses, burnt and bare,
    Crushed it beneath their tread,
Or Pharaoh's flashing wheels into the air
    Scattered it as they sped ;

Or Mary, with the Christ of Nazareth
    Held close in her caress,
Whose pilgrimage of hope and love and
        faith
    Illumed the wilderness ;

Or anchorites beneath Engaddi's palms
    Pacing the Dead Sea beach,
And singing slow their old Armenian
        psalms
    In half-articulate speech ;

Or caravans, that from Bassora's gate
    With westward steps depart ;
Or Mecca's pilgrims, confident of Fate,
    And resolute in heart !

These have passed over it, or may have
    passed !
    Now in this crystal tower
Imprisoned by some curious hand at last,
    It counts the passing hour.

And as I gaze, these narrow walls ex-
    pand ; —
    Before my dreamy eye
Stretches the desert with its shifting sand,
    Its unimpeded sky.

And borne aloft by the sustaining blast,
    This little golden thread
Dilates into a column high and vast,
    A form of fear and dread.

And onward, and across the setting sun,
    Across the boundless plain,
The column and its broader shadow run,
    Till thought pursues in vain.

The vision vanishes! These walls again
   Shut out the lurid sun,
Shut out the hot, immeasurable plain;
   The half-hour's sand is run!

KING WITLAF'S DRINKING-HORN.

ITLAF, a king of the Saxons,
   Ere yet his last he breathed,
   To the merry monks of Croyland
His drinking-horn bequeathed, —

That, whenever they sat at their revels,
   And drank from the golden bowl,
They might remember the donor,
   And breathe a prayer for his soul.

So sat they once at Christmas,
   And bade the goblet pass;
In their beards the red wine glistened
   Like dew-drops in the grass.

They drank to the soul of Witlaf,
   They drank to Christ the Lord,
And to each of the Twelve Apostles,
   Who had preached his holy word.

They drank to the Saints and Martyrs
    Of the dismal days of yore,
And as soon as the horn was empty
    They remembered one Saint more.

And the reader droned from the pulpit,
    Like the murmur of many bees,
The legend of good Saint Guthlac,
    And Saint Basil's homilies ;

Till the great bells of the convent,
    From their prison in the tower,
Guthlac and Bartholomæus,
    Proclaimed the midnight hour.

And the Yule-log cracked in the chimney,
    And the Abbot bowed his head,
And the flamelets flapped and flickered,
    But the Abbot was stark and dead.

Yet still in his pallid fingers
    He clutched the golden bowl,
In which, like a pearl dissolving,
    Had sunk and dissolved his soul.

But not for this their revels
    The jovial monks forbore,

For they cried, " Fill high the goblet !
We must drink to one Saint more ! "

❧

THE SINGERS.

OD sent his Singers upon earth
With songs of sadness and of
mirth,
That they might touch the hearts of men,
And bring them back to heaven again.

The first, a youth with soul of fire,
Held in his hand a golden lyre ;
Through groves he wandered, and by
streams,
Playing the music of our dreams.

The second, with a bearded face,
Stood singing in the market-place,
And stirred with accents deep and loud
The hearts of all the listening crowd.

A gray old man, the third and last,
Sang in cathedrals dim and vast,
While the majestic organ rolled
Contrition from its mouths of gold.

And those who heard the Singers three
Disputed which the best might be ;
For still their music seemed to start
Discordant echoes in each heart.

But the great Master said, " I see
No best in kind, but in degree ;
I gave a various gift to each,
To charm, to strengthen, and to teach.

" These are the three great chords of
      might,
And he whose ear is tuned aright
Will hear no discord in the three,
But the most perfect harmony."

PROMETHEUS,

OR THE POET'S FORETHOUGHT.

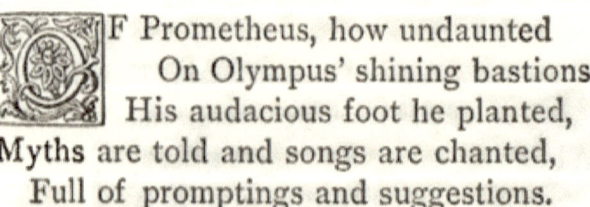F Prometheus, how undaunted
      On Olympus' shining bastions
      His audacious foot he planted,
Myths are told and songs are chanted,
   Full of promptings and suggestions.

Beautiful is the tradition
  Of that flight through heavenly portals,
The old classic superstition
Of the theft and the transmission
  Of the fire of the Immortals!

First the deed of noble daring,
  Born of heavenward aspiration,
Then the fire with mortals sharing,
Then the vulture, — the despairing
  Cry of pain on crags Caucasian.

All is but a symbol painted
  Of the Poet, Prophet, Seer ;
Only those are crowned and sainted
Who with grief have been acquainted,
  Making nations nobler, freer.

In their feverish exultations,
  In their triumph and their yearning,
In their passionate pulsations,
In their words among the nations,
  The Promethean fire is burning.

Shall it, then, be unavailing,
  All this toil for human culture ?
Through the cloud-rack, dark and trailing

Must they see above them sailing
  O'er life's barren crags the vulture?

Such a fate as this was Dante's,
  By defeat and exile maddened;
Thus were Milton and Cervantes,
Nature's priests and Corybantes,
  By affliction touched and saddened.

But the glories so transcendent
  That around their memories cluster,
And, on all their steps attendant,
Make their darkened lives resplendent
  With such gleams of inward lustre!

All the melodies mysterious,
  Through the dreary darkness chanted;
Thoughts in attitudes imperious,
Voices soft, and deep, and serious,
  Words   that   whispered,   songs   that
      haunted!

All the soul in rapt suspension,
  All the quivering, palpitating
Chords of life in utmost tension,
With the fervor of invention,
  With the rapture of creating!

Ah, Prometheus! heaven-scaling!
　　In such hours of exultation
Even the faintest heart, unquailing,
Might behold the vulture sailing
　　Round the cloudy crags Caucasian!

Though to all there be not given
　　Strength for such sublime endeavor,
Thus to scale the walls of heaven,
And to leaven with fiery leaven,
　　All the hearts of men forever;

Yet all bards, whose hearts unblighted
　　Honor and believe the presage,
Hold aloft their torches lighted,
Gleaming through the realms benighted,
　　As they onward bear the message!

EPIMETHEUS,

OR THE POET'S AFTERTHOUGHT.

AVE I dreamed? or was it real,
　　What I saw as in a vision,
　　When to marches hymeneal
In the land of the Ideal
　　Moved my thought o'er Fields Elysian?

What! are these the guests whose glances
   Seemed like sunshine gleaming round
      me?
These the wild, bewildering fancies,
That with dithyrambic dances
   As with magic circles bound me?

Ah! how cold are their caresses!
   Pallid cheeks, and haggard bosoms!
Spectral gleam their snow-white dresses,
And from loose, dishevelled tresses
   Fall the hyacinthine blossoms!

O my songs! whose winsome measures
   Filled my heart with secret rapture!
Children of my golden leisures!
Must even your delights and pleasures
   Fade and perish with the capture?

Fair they seemed, those songs sonorous,
   When they came to me unbidden;
Voices single, and in chorus,
Like the wild birds singing o'er us
   In the dark of branches hidden.

Disenchantment! Disillusion!
   Must each noble aspiration

Come at last to this conclusion,
Jarring discord, wild confusion,
  Lassitude, renunciation ?

Not with steeper fall nor faster,
  From the sun's serene dominions,
Not through brighter realms nor vaster,
In swift ruin and disaster,
  Icarus fell with shattered pinions !

Sweet Pandora ! dear Pandora !
  Why did mighty Jove create thee
Coy as Thetis, fair as Flora,
Beautiful as young Aurora,
  If to win thee is to hate thee ?

No, not hate thee ! for this feeling
  Of unrest and long resistance
Is but passionate appealing,
A prophetic whisper stealing
  O'er the chords of our existence.

Him whom thou dost once enamor,
  Thou, beloved, never leavest ;
In life's discord, strife, and clamor,
Still he feels thy spell of glamour ;
  Him of Hope thou ne'er bereavest.

Weary hearts by thee are lifted,
  Struggling souls by thee are strength-
     ened,
Clouds of fear asunder rifted,
Truth from falsehood cleansed and sifted,
  Lives, like days in summer, lengthened !

Therefore art thou ever dearer,
  O my Sibyl, my deceiver !
For thou makest each mystery clearer,
And the unattained seems nearer,
  When thou fillest my heart with fever !

Muse of all the Gifts and Graces !
  Though the fields around us wither,
There are ampler realms and spaces,
Where no foot has left its traces :
  Let us turn and wander thither !

THE LADDER OF ST. AUGUSTINE.

SAINT AUGUSTINE ! well hast
    thou said,
    That of our vices we can frame
A ladder, if we will but tread
  Beneath our feet each deed of shame !

All common things, each day's events,
  That with the hour begin and end,
Our pleasures and our discontents,
  Are rounds by which we may ascend.

The low desire, the base design,
  That makes another's virtues less;
The revel of the ruddy wine,
  And all occasions of excess;

The longing for ignoble things;
  The strife for triumph more than truth;
The hardening of the heart, that brings
  Irreverence for the dreams of youth;

All thoughts of ill; all evil deeds,
  That have their root in thoughts of ill;
Whatever hinders or impedes
  The action of the nobler will; —

All these must first be trampled down
  Beneath our feet, if we would gain
In the bright fields of fair renown
  The right of eminent domain.

We have not wings, we cannot soar;
  But we have feet to scale and climb

By slow degrees, by more and more,
   The cloudy summits of our time.

The mighty pyramids of stone
   That wedge-like cleave the desert airs,
When nearer seen, and better known,
   Are but gigantic flights of stairs.

The distant mountains, that uprear
   Their solid bastions to the skies,
Are crossed by pathways, that appear
   As we to higher levels rise.

The heights by great men reached and
      kept
   Were not attained by sudden flight,
But they, while their companions slept,
   Were toiling upward in the night.

Standing on what too long we bore
   With shoulders bent and downcast eyes,
We may discern — unseen before —
   A path to higher destinies,

Nor deem the irrevocable Past
   As wholly wasted, wholly vain,
If, rising on its wrecks, at last
   To something nobler we attain.

THE PHANTOM SHIP.

IN Mather's Magnalia Christi,
　　Of the old colonial time,
　May be found in prose the legend
　That is here set down in rhyme.

A ship sailed from New Haven,
　And the keen and frosty airs,
That filled her sails at parting,
　Were heavy with good men's prayers.

"O Lord ! if it be thy pleasure " —
　Thus prayed the old divine —
" To bury our friends in the ocean,
　Take them, for they are thine ! "

But Master Lamberton muttered,
　And under his breath said he,
"This ship is so crank and walty,
　I fear our grave she will be ! "

And the ships that came from England,
　When the winter months were gone,
Brought no tidings of this vessel
　Nor of Master Lamberton.

This put the people to praying
  That the Lord would let them hear
What in his greater wisdom
  He had done with friends so dear.

And at last their prayers were answered :
  It was in the month of June,
An hour before the sunset
  Of a windy afternoon,

When, steadily steering landward,
  A ship was seen below,
And they knew it was Lamberton, Master,
  Who sailed so long ago.

On she came, with a cloud of canvas,
  Right against the wind that blew,
Until the eye could distinguish
  The faces of the crew.

Then fell her straining topmasts,
  Hanging tangled in the shrouds,
And her sails were loosened and lifted,
  And blown away like clouds.

And the masts, with all their rigging,
  Fell slowly, one by one,

And the hulk dilated and vanished,
  As a sea-mist in the sun !

And the people who saw this marvel
  Each said unto his friend,
That this was the mould of their vessel,
  And thus her tragic end.

And the pastor of the village
  Gave thanks to God in prayer,
That, to quiet their troubled spirits,
  He had sent this Ship of Air.

THE WARDEN OF THE CINQUE PORTS.

 MIST was driving down the
      British Channel,
  The day was just begun,
And through the window-panes, on floor
    and panel,
  Streamed the red autumn sun.

It glanced on flowing flag and rippling
    pennon,
  And the white sails of ships ;

And, from the frowning rampart, the black
    cannon
  Hailed it with feverish lips.

Sandwich and Romney, Hastings, Hithe,
    and Dover
  Were all alert that day,
To see the French war-steamers speeding
    over,
  When the fog cleared away.

Sullen and silent, and like couchant lions,
  Their cannon, through the night,
Holding their breath, had watched, in
    grim defiance,
  The sea-coast opposite.

And now they roared at drum-beat from
    their stations
  On every citadel;
Each answering each, with morning salu-
    tations,
  That all was well.

And down the coast, all taking up the
    burden,
  Replied the distant forts,

As if to summon from his sleep the
    Warden
And Lord of the Cinque Ports.

Him shall no sunshine from the fields of
    azure,
    No drum-beat from the wall,
No morning gun from the black fort's
    embrasure,
    Awaken with its call!

No more, surveying with an eye impartial
    The long line of the coast,
Shall the gaunt figure of the old Field
    Marshal
    Be seen upon his post!

For in the night, unseen, a single warrior,
    In sombre harness mailed,
Dreaded of man, and surnamed the De-
    stroyer,
    The rampart wall had scaled.

He passed into the chamber of the
    sleeper,
    The dark and silent room,

And as he entered, darker grew, and
    deeper,
    The silence and the gloom.

He did not pause to parley or dissemble,
    But smote the Warden hoar ;
Ah ! what a blow ! that made all England
    tremble
    And groan from shore to shore.

Meanwhile, without, the surly cannon
    waited,
    The sun rose bright o'erhead ;
Nothing in Nature's aspect intimated
    That a great man was dead.

THE JEWISH CEMETERY AT NEWPORT.

HOW strange it seems ! These He-
    brews in their graves,
    Close by the street of this fair
    seaport town,
Silent beside the never-silent waves,
    At rest in all this moving up and down !

The trees are white with dust, that o'er
    their sleep
  Wave their broad curtains in the south-
    wind's breath,
While underneath these leafy tents they
    keep
  The long, mysterious Exodus of Death.

And these sepulchral stones, so old and
    brown,
  That pave with level flags their burial-
    place,
Seem like the tablets of the Law, thrown
    down
  And broken by Moses at the mountain's
    base.

The very names recorded here are strange,
  Of foreign accent, and of different
    climes ;
Alvares and Rivera interchange
  With Abraham and Jacob of old times.

" Blessed be God ! for he created Death ! "
  The mourners said, "and Death is rest
    and peace ; "

Then added, in the certainty of faith,
  "And giveth Life that nevermore shall
    cease."

Closed are the portals of their Synagogue,
  No Psalms of David now the silence
    break,
No Rabbi reads the ancient Decalogue
  In the grand dialect the Prophets spake.

Gone are the living, but the dead remain,
  And not neglected ; for a hand unseen,
Scattering its bounty, like a summer rain,
  Still keeps their graves and their re-
    membrance green.

How came they here ?   What burst of
    Christian hate,
  What persecution, merciless and blind,
Drove o'er the sea — that desert deso-
    late —
  These Ishmaels and Hagars of man-
    kind ?

They lived in narrow streets and lanes
    obscure,
  Ghetto and Judenstrass, in mirk and
    mire ;

Taught in the school of patience to endure
  The life of anguish and the death of
    fire.

All their lives long, with the unleavened
    bread
  And bitter herbs of exile and its fears,
The wasting famine of the heart they fed,
  And slaked its thirst with marah of their
    tears.

Anathema maranatha! was the cry
  That rang from town to town, from street
    to street;
At every gate the accursed Mordecai
  Was mocked and jeered, and spurned
    by Christian feet.

Pride and humiliation hand in hand
  Walked with them through the world
    where'er they went;
Trampled and beaten were they as the
    sand,
  And yet unshaken as the continent.

For in the background figures vague and
    vast

Of patriarchs and of prophets rose sub-
lime,
And all the great traditions of the Past
They saw reflected in the coming time.

And thus forever with reverted look
The mystic volume of the world they
read,
Spelling it backward, like a Hebrew book,
Till life became a Legend of the Dead.

But ah! what once has been shall be no
more!
The groaning earth in travail and in
pain
Brings forth its races, but does not restore,
And the dead nations never rise again.

OLIVER BASSELIN.

N the Valley of the Vire
Still is seen an ancient mill,
With its gables quaint and queer,
And beneath the window-sill,
On the stone,
These words alone:
"Oliver Basselin lived here."

Far above it, on the steep,
  Ruined stands the old Château ;
Nothing but the donjon-keep
  Left for shelter or for show.
      Its vacant eyes
      Stare at the skies,
Stare at the valley green and deep.

Once a convent, old and brown,
  Looked, but ah ! it looks no more,
From the neighboring hillside down
  On the rushing and the roar
      Of the stream
      Whose sunny gleam
Cheers the little Norman town.

In that darksome mill of stone,
  To the water's dash and din,
Careless, humble, and unknown,
  Sang the poet Basselin
      Songs that fill
      That ancient mill
With a splendor of its own.

Never feeling of unrest
  Broke the pleasant dream he dreamed ;
Only made to be his nest,
  All the lovely valley seemed ;

No desire
Of soaring higher
Stirred or fluttered in his breast.

True, his songs were not divine ;
    Were not songs of that high art,
Which, as winds do in the pine,
    Find an answer in each heart ;
        But the mirth
        Of this green earth
Laughed and revelled in his line.

From the alehouse and the inn,
    Opening on the narrow street,
Came the loud, convivial din,
    Singing and applause of feet,
        The laughing lays
        That in those days
Sang the poet Basselin.

In the castle, cased in steel,
    Knights, who fought at Agincourt,
Watched and waited, spur on heel ;
    But the poet sang for sport
        Songs that rang
        Another clang,
Songs that lowlier hearts could feel.

In the convent, clad in gray,
  Sat the monks in lonely cells,
Paced the cloisters, knelt to pray,
  And the poet heard their bells ;
      But his rhymes
      Found other chimes,
Nearer to the earth than they.

Gone are all the barons bold,
  Gone are all the knights and squires,
Gone the abbot stern and cold,
  And the brotherhood of friars ;
      Not a name
      Remains to fame,
From those mouldering days of old !

But the poet's memory here
  Of the landscape makes a part ;
Like the river, swift and clear,
  Flows his song through many a heart ;
      Haunting still
      That ancient mill
In the Valley of the Vire.

VICTOR GALBRAITH.

NDER the walls of Monterey
At daybreak the bugles began to
    play,
Victor Galbraith !
In the mist of the morning damp and gray,
These were the words they seemed to say :
    "Come forth to thy death,
        Victor Galbraith ! "

Forth he came, with a martial tread ;
Firm was his step, erect his head ;
        Victor Galbraith,
He who so well the bugle played,
Could not mistake the words it said :
    "Come forth to thy death,
        Victor Galbraith ! "

He looked at the earth, he looked at the
    sky,
He looked at the files of musketry,
        Victor Galbraith !
And he said, with a steady voice and eye,
"Take good aim ; I am ready to die ! "
        Thus challenges death
        Victor Galbraith.

Twelve fiery tongues flashed straight and
     red,
Six leaden balls on their errand sped ;
       Victor Galbraith
Falls to the ground, but he is not dead :
His name was not stamped on those balls
     of lead,
       And they only scath
       Victor Galbraith.

Three balls are in his breast and brain,
But he rises out of the dust again,
       Victor Galbraith !
The water he drinks has a bloody stain ;
" Oh kill me, and put me out of my pain ! "
       In his agony prayeth
       Victor Galbraith !

Forth dart once more those tongues of
     flame,
And the bugler has died a death of shame,
       Victor Galbraith !
His soul has gone back to whence it came,
And no one answers to the name,
       When the Sergeant saith,
       " Victor Galbraith ! "

Under the walls of Monterey
By night a bugle is heard to play,
  Victor Galbraith!
Through the mist of the valley damp and
  gray
The sentinels hear the sound, and say,
  "That is the wraith
   Of Victor Galbraith!"

MY LOST YOUTH.

FTEN **I** think of the beautiful
  town
  That is seated by the sea;
Often in thought go up and down
The pleasant streets of that dear old town,
 And my youth comes back to me.
  And a verse of a Lapland song
  Is haunting my memory still:
 "A boy's will is the wind's will,
And the thoughts of youth are long, long
  thoughts."

I can see the shadowy lines of its trees,
 And catch, in sudden gleams,

The sheen of the far-surrounding seas,
And islands that were the Hesperides
  Of all my boyish dreams.
    And the burden of that old song,
    It murmurs and whispers still :
  " A boy's will is the wind's will,
And the thoughts of youth are long, long
    thoughts."

I remember the black wharves and the
    slips,
  And the sea-tides tossing free ;
And Spanish sailors with bearded lips,
And the beauty and mystery of the ships,
  And the magic of the sea.
    And the voice of that wayward song
    Is singing and saying still :
  " A boy's will is the wind's will,
And the thoughts of youth are long, long
    thoughts."

I remember the bulwarks by the shore,
  And the fort upon the hill ;
The sunrise gun, with its hollow roar,
The drum-beat repeated o'er and o'er,
  And the bugle wild and shrill.
    And the music of that old song

Throbs in my memory still :
" A boy's will is the wind's will,
And the thoughts of youth are long, long
    thoughts."

I remember the sea-fight far away,
    How it thundered o'er the tide !
And the dead captains, as they lay
In their graves, o'erlooking the tranquil
    bay,
    Where they in battle died.
      And the sound of that mournful song
      Goes through me with a thrill :
" A boy's will is the wind's will,
And the thoughts of youth are long, long
    thoughts."

I can see the breezy dome of groves,
    The shadows of Deering's Woods ;
And the friendships old and the early
    loves
Come back with a Sabbath sound, as of
    doves
    In quiet neighborhoods.
      And the verse of that sweet old song,
      It flutters and murmurs still :
    " A boy's will is the wind's will,

And the thoughts of youth are long, long
    thoughts."

I remember the gleams and glooms that
    dart
  Across the school-boy's brain ;
The song and the silence in the heart,
That in part are prophecies, and in part
  Are longings wild and vain.
    And the voice of that fitful song
    Sings on, and is never still :
  " A boy's will is the wind's will,
And the thoughts of youth are long, long
    thoughts."

There are things of which I may not
    speak ;
  There are dreams that cannot die ;
There are thoughts that make the strong
    heart weak,
And bring a pallor into the cheek,
  And a mist before the eye.
    And the words of that fatal song
    Come over me like a chill :
  " A boy's will is the wind's will,
And the thoughts of youth are long, long
    thoughts."

Strange to me now are the forms I meet
  When I visit the dear old town ;
But the native air is pure and sweet,
And the trees that o'ershadow each well-
      known street,
  As they balance up and down,
    Are singing the beautiful song,
    Are sighing and whispering still :
 " A boy's will is the wind's will,
And the thoughts of youth are long, long
      thoughts."

And Deering's Woods are fresh and fair,
  And with joy that is almost pain
My heart goes back to wander there,
And among the dreams of the days that
      were,
  I find my lost youth again.
    And the strange and beautiful song,
    The groves are repeating it still :
 " A boy's will is the wind's will,
And the thoughts of youth are long, long
      thoughts."

THE ROPEWALK.

IN that building, long and low,
  With its windows all a-row,
    Like the port-holes of a hulk,
Human spiders spin and spin,
Backward down their threads so thin
  Dropping, each a hempen bulk.

At the end, an open door ;
Squares of sunshine on the floor
  Light the long and dusky lane ;
And the whirring of a wheel,
Dull and drowsy, makes me feel
  All its spokes are in my brain.

As the spinners to the end
Downward go and reascend,
  Gleam the long threads in the sun ;
While within this brain of mine
Cobwebs brighter and more fine
  By the busy wheel are spun.

Two fair maidens in a swing,
Like white doves upon the wing,
  First before my vision pass ;

Laughing, as their gentle hands
Closely clasp the twisted strands,
    At their shadow on the grass.

Then a booth of mountebanks,
With its smell of tan and planks,
    And a girl poised high in air
On a cord, in spangled dress,
With a faded loveliness,
    And a weary look of care.

Then a homestead among farms,
And a woman with bare arms
    Drawing water from a well ;
As the bucket mounts apace,
With it mounts her own fair face,
    As at some magician's spell.

Then an old man in a tower,
Ringing loud the noontide hour,
    While the rope coils round and round
Like a serpent at his feet,
And again, in swift retreat,
    Nearly lifts him from the ground.

Then within a prison-yard,
Faces fixed, and stern, and hard,

Laughter and indecent mirth ;
Ah ! it is the gallows-tree !
Breath of Christian charity,
   Blow, and sweep it from the earth !

Then a school-boy, with his kite
Gleaming in a sky of light,
   And an eager, upward look ;
Steeds pursued through lane and field ;
Fowlers with their snares concealed ;
   And an angler, by a brook.

Ships rejoicing in the breeze,
Wrecks that float o'er unknown seas,
   Anchors dragged through faithless
      sand ;
Sea-fog drifting overhead,
And, with lessening line and lead,
   Sailors feeling for the land.

All these scenes do I behold,
These, and many left untold,
   In that building long and low ;
While the wheel goes round and round,
With a drowsy, dreamy sound,
   And the spinners backward go.

THE GOLDEN MILE-STONE.

EAFLESS are the trees; their
purple branches
Spread themselves abroad, like
reefs of coral,
Rising silent
In the Red Sea of the winter sunset.

From the hundred chimneys of the vil-
lage,
Like the Afreet in the Arabian story,
Smoky columns
Tower aloft into the air of amber.

At the window winks the flickering fire-
light;
Here and there the lamps of evening
glimmer,
Social watch-fires
Answering one another through the darkness.

On the hearth the lighted logs are glow-
ing,
And like Ariel in the cloven pine-tree

For its freedom
Groans and sighs the air imprisoned in
them.

By the fireside there are old men seated,
Seeing ruined cities in the ashes,
Asking sadly
Of the Past what it can ne'er restore
them.

By the fireside there are youthful dream-
ers,
Building castles fair, with stately stair-
ways,
Asking blindly
Of the Future what it cannot give them.

By the fireside tragedies are acted
In whose scenes appear two actors only,
Wife and husband,
And above them God the sole spectator.

By the fireside there are peace and com-
fort,
Wives and children, with fair, thoughtful
faces,
Waiting, watching
For a well-known footstep in the passage.

Each man's chimney is his Golden Mile-
    Stone ;
Is the central point, from which he meas-
    ures
        Every distance
Through the gateways of the world around
    him.

In his farthest wanderings still he sees it ;
Hears the talking flame, the answering
    night-wind,
        As he heard them
When he sat with those who were, but are
    not.

Happy he whom neither wealth nor
    fashion,
Nor the march of the encroaching city,
        Drives an exile
From the hearth of his ancestral home-
    stead.

We may build more splendid habitations,
Fill our rooms with paintings and with
    sculptures,
        But we cannot
Buy with gold the old associations !

SANTA FILOMENA.

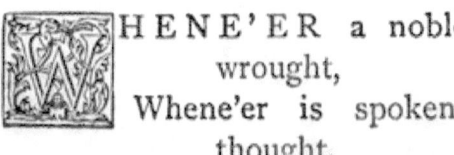HENE'ER a noble deed is
      wrought,
   Whene'er is spoken a noble
      thought,
Our hearts, in glad surprise,
To higher levels rise.

The tidal wave of deeper souls
Into our inmost being rolls,
   And lifts us unawares
   Out of all meaner cares.

Honor to those whose words or deeds
Thus help us in our daily needs,
   And by their overflow
   Raise us from what is low !

Thus thought I, as by night I read
Of the great army of the dead,
   The trenches cold and damp,
   The starved and frozen camp, —

The wounded from the battle-plain,
In dreary hospitals of pain,

The cheerless corridors,
The cold and stony floors.

Lo ! in that house of misery
A lady with a lamp I see
    Pass through the glimmering gloom,
    And flit from room to room.

And slow, as in a dream of bliss,
The speechless sufferer turns to kiss
    Her shadow, as it falls
    Upon the darkening walls.

As if a door in heaven should be
Opened and then closed suddenly,
    The vision came and went,
    The light shone and was spent.

On England's annals, through the long
Hereafter of her speech and song,
    That light its rays shall cast
    From portals of the past.

A Lady with a Lamp shall stand
In the great history of the land,
    A noble type of good,
    Heroic womanhood.

Nor even shall be wanting here
The palm, the lily, and the spear,
The symbols that of yore
Saint Filomena bore.

DAYBREAK.

 WIND came up out of the sea,
And said, "O mists, make room
for me."

It hailed the ships, and cried, "Sail on,
Ye mariners, the night is gone."

And hurried landward far away,
Crying, "Awake! it is the day."

It said unto the forest, "Shout!
Hang all your leafy banners out!"

It touched the wood-bird's folded wing,
And said, "O bird, awake and sing."

And o'er the farms, "O chanticleer,
Your clarion blow; the day is near."

It whispered to the fields of corn,
"Bow down, and hail the coming morn."

It shouted through the belfry-tower,
"Awake, O bell! proclaim the hour."

It crossed the churchyard with a sigh,
And said, "Not yet! in quiet lie."

THE FIFTIETH BIRTHDAY OF AGASSIZ.

MAY 28, 1857.

T was fifty years ago
  In the pleasant month of May,
  In the beautiful Pays de Vaud,
   A child in its cradle lay.

And Nature, the old nurse, took
  The child upon her knee,
Saying : " Here is a story-book
  Thy Father has written for thee."

" Come, wander with me," she said,
  " Into regions yet untrod ;
And read what is still unread
  In the manuscripts of God."

And he wandered away and away
  With Nature, the dear old nurse,
Who sang to him night and day
  The rhymes of the universe.

And whenever the way seemed long,
  Or his heart began to fail,
She would sing a more wonderful song,
  Or tell a more marvellous tale.

So she keeps him still a child,
  And will not let him go,
Though at times his heart beats wild
  For the beautiful Pays de Vaud ;

Though at times he hears in his dreams
  The Ranz des Vaches of old,
And the rush of mountain streams
  From glaciers clear and cold ;

And the mother at home says, " Hark !
  For his voice I listen and yearn ;
It is growing late and dark,
  And my boy does not return ! "

THE CHILDREN'S HOUR.

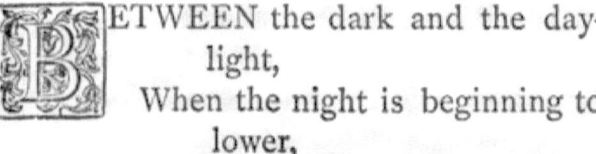ETWEEN the dark and the day-
    light,
  When the night is beginning to
    lower,
Comes a pause in the day's occupations,
  That is known as the Children's Hour.

I hear in the chamber above me
  The patter of little feet,
The sound of a door that is opened,
  And voices soft and sweet.

From my study I see in the lamplight,
  Descending the broad hall stair,
Grave Alice, and laughing Allegra,
  And Edith with golden hair.

A whisper, and then a silence :
  Yet I know by their merry eyes
They are plotting and planning together
  To take me by surprise.

A sudden rush from the stairway,
  A sudden raid from the hall !

By three doors left unguarded
　They enter my castle wall!

They climb up into my turret
　O'er the arms and back of my chair;
If I try to escape, they surround me;
　They seem to be everywhere.

They almost devour me with kisses,
　Their arms about me entwine,
Till I think of the Bishop of Bingen
　In his Mouse-Tower on the Rhine!

Do you think, O blue-eyed banditti,
　Because you have scaled the wall,
Such an old mustache as I am
　Is not a match for you all!

I have you fast in my fortress,
　And will not let you depart,
But put you down into the dungeon
　In the round-tower of my heart.

And there will I keep you forever,
　Yes, forever and a day,
Till the walls shall crumble to ruin,
　And moulder in dust away!

ENCELADUS.

UNDER Mount Etna he lies,
    It is slumber, it is not death ;
    For he struggles at times to arise,
And above him the lurid skies
    Are hot with his fiery breath.

The crags are piled on his breast,
    The earth is heaped on his head ;
But the groans of his wild unrest,
Though smothered and half suppressed,
    Are heard, and he is not dead.

And the nations far away
    Are watching with eager eyes ;
They talk together and say,
" To-morrow, perhaps to-day,
    Enceladus will arise ! "

And the old gods, the austere
    Oppressors in their strength,
Stand aghast and white with fear
At the ominous sounds they hear,
    And tremble, and mutter, " At length ! "

Ah me ! for the land that is sown
　With the harvest of despair !
Where the burning cinders, blown
From the lips of the overthrown
　Enceladus, fill the air.

Where ashes are heaped in drifts
　Over vineyard and field and town,
Whenever he starts and lifts
His head through the blackened rifts
　Of the crags that keep him down.

See, see ! the red light shines !
　'T is the glare of his awful eyes !
And the storm-wind shouts through the
　　　pines
Of Alps and of Apennines,
　" Enceladus, arise ! "

PAUL REVERE'S RIDE.

ISTEN, my children, and you
　　　shall hear
Of the midnight ride of Paul
　　　Revere,
On the eighteenth of April, in Seventy-
　　five ;

Hardly a man is now alive
Who remembers that famous day and
    year.

He said to his friend, " If the British
    march
By land or sea from the town to-night,
Hang a lantern aloft in the belfry arch
Of the North Church tower as a signal
    light, —
One, if by land, and two, if by sea ;
And I on the opposite shore will be,
Ready to ride and spread the alarm
Through every Middlesex village and
    farm,
For the country folk to be up and to arm."

Then he said, "Good night!" and with
    muffled oar
Silently rowed to the Charlestown shore,
Just as the moon rose over the bay,
Where swinging wide at her moorings lay
The Somerset, British man-of-war ;
A phantom ship, with each mast and spar
Across the moon like a prison bar,
And a huge black hulk, that was magnified
By its own reflection in the tide.

Meanwhile, his friend, through alley and
    street,
Wanders and watches with eager ears,
Till in the silence around him he hears
The muster of men at the barrack door,
The sound of arms, and the tramp of feet,
And the measured tread of the grenadiers,
Marching down to their boats on the
    shore.

Then he climbed the tower of the Old
    North Church,
By the wooden stairs, with stealthy tread,
To the belfry-chamber overhead,
And startled the pigeons from their perch
On the sombre rafters, that round him
    made
Masses and moving shapes of shade, —
By the trembling ladder, steep and tall,
To the highest window in the wall,
Where he paused to listen and look down
A moment on the roofs of the town,
And the moonlight flowing over all.

Beneath, in the churchyard, lay the dead,
In their night-encampment on the hill,
Wrapped in silence so deep and still
That he could hear, like a sentinel's tread,

The watchful night-wind, as it went
Creeping along from tent to tent,
And seeming to whisper, " All is well ! "
A moment only he feels the spell
Of the place and the hour, and the secret
      dread
Of the lonely belfry and the dead ;
For suddenly all his thoughts are bent
On a shadowy something far away,
Where the river widens to meet the bay, —
A line of black that bends and floats
On the rising tide, like a bridge of boats.

Meanwhile, impatient to mount and ride,
Booted and spurred, with a heavy stride
On the opposite shore walked Paul
      Revere.
Now he patted his horse's side,
Now gazed at the landscape far and near,
Then, impetuous, stamped the earth,
And turned and tightened his saddle-
      girth ;
But mostly he watched with eager search
The belfry-tower of the Old North Church,
As it rose above the graves on the hill,
Lonely and spectral and sombre and still.
And lo ! as he looks, on the belfry's
      height

A glimmer, and then a gleam of light!
He springs to the saddle, the bridle he
      turns,
But lingers and gazes, till full on his sight
A second lamp in the belfry burns!

A hurry of hoofs in a village street,
A shape in the moonlight, a bulk in the
      dark,
And beneath, from the pebbles, in pass-
      ing, a spark
Struck out by a steed flying fearless and
      fleet:
That was all! And yet, through the gloom
      and the light,
The fate of a nation was riding that night;
And the spark struck out by that steed, in
      his flight,
Kindled the land into flame with its heat.

He has left the village and mounted the
      steep,
And beneath him, tranquil and broad and
      deep,
Is the Mystic, meeting the ocean tides;
And under the alders, that skirt its edge,
Now soft on the sand, now loud on the
      ledge,

Is heard the tramp of his steed as he
    rides.

It was twelve by the village clock,
When he crossed the bridge into Medford
        town.
He heard the crowing of the cock,
And the barking of the farmer's dog,
And felt the damp of the river fog,
That rises after the sun goes down.

It was one by the village clock,
When he galloped into Lexington.
He saw the gilded weathercock
Swim in the moonlight as he passed,
And the meeting-house windows, blank
        and bare,
Gaze at him with a spectral glare,
As if they already stood aghast
At the bloody work they would look upon.

It was two by the village clock,
When he came to the bridge in Concord
        town.
He heard the bleating of the flock,
And the twitter of birds among the trees,
And felt the breath of the morning breeze
Blowing over the meadows brown.

And one was safe and asleep in his bed
Who at the bridge would be first to fall,
Who that day would be lying dead,
Pierced by a British musket-ball.

You know the rest. In the books you
    have read,
How the British Regulars fired and
    fled, —
How the farmers gave them ball for ball,
From behind each fence and farm-yard
    wall,
Chasing the red-coats down the lane,
Then crossing the fields to emerge again
Under the trees at the turn of the road,
And only pausing to fire and load.

So through the night rode Paul Revere ;
And so through the night went his cry of
    alarm
To every Middlesex village and farm, —
A cry of defiance and not of fear,
A voice in the darkness, a knock at the
    door,
And a word that shall echo forevermore !
For, borne on the night-wind of the Past,
Through all our history, to the last,

In the hour of darkness and peril and
 need,
The people will waken and listen to hear
The hurrying hoof-beats of that steed,
And the midnight message of Paul
 Revere.

KING ROBERT OF SICILY.

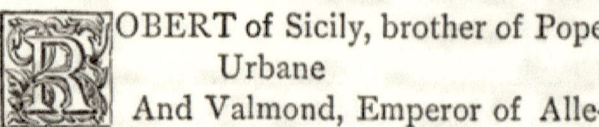

OBERT of Sicily, brother of Pope
 Urbane
 And Valmond, Emperor of Alle-
 maine,
Apparelled in magnificent attire,
With retinue of many a knight and squire,
On St. John's eve, at vespers proudly sat,
And heard the priests chant the Magni-
 ficat.
And as he listened, o'er and o'er again
Repeated, like a burden or refrain,
He caught the words, " *Deposuit potentes
De sede, et exaltavit humiles ;* "
And slowly lifting up his kingly head,
He to a learned clerk beside him said,
" What mean these words ? " The clerk
 made answer meet,

" He has put down the mighty from their
  seat,
And has exalted them of low degree."
Thereat King Robert muttered scornfully,
" 'T is well that such seditious words are
  sung
Only by priests and in the Latin tongue;
For unto priests and people be it known,
There is no power can push me from my
  throne ! "
And leaning back, he yawned and fell
  asleep,
Lulled by the chant monotonous and
  deep.

When he awoke, it was already night ;
The church was empty, and there was no
  light,
Save where the lamps, that glimmered few
  and faint,
Lighted a little space before some saint.
He started from his seat and gazed
  around,
But saw no living thing and heard no
  sound.
He groped towards the door, but it was
  locked ;

He cried aloud, and listened, and then
    knocked,
And uttered awful threatenings and com-
    plaints,
And imprecations upon men and saints.
The sounds reëchoed from the roof and
    walls
As if dead priests were laughing in their
    stalls.

At length the sexton, hearing from with-
    out
The tumult of the knocking and the
    shout,
And thinking thieves were in the house of
    prayer,
Came with his lantern, asking, " Who is
    there ? "
Half choked with rage, King Robert
    fiercely said,
"Open : 't is I, the King !   Art thou
    afraid ? "
The frightened sexton, muttering, with a
    curse,
" This is some drunken vagabond, or
    worse ! "
Turned the great key and flung the portal
    wide ;

A man rushed by him at a single stride,
Haggard, half naked, without hat or
    cloak,
Who neither turned, nor looked at him,
    nor spoke,
But leaped into the blackness of the
    night,
And vanished like a spectre from his
    sight.

Robert of Sicily, brother of Pope Urbane
And Valmond, Emperor of Allemaine,
Despoiled of his magnificent attire,
Bareheaded, breathless, and besprent with
    mire,
With sense of wrong and outrage desper-
    ate,
Strode on and thundered at the palace
    gate;
Rushed through the courtyard, thrusting
    in his rage
To right and left each seneschal and page,
And hurried up the broad and sounding
    stair,
His white face ghastly in the torches'
    glare.
From hall to hall he passed with breath-
    less speed;

Voices and cries he heard, but did not
    heed,
Until at last he reached the banquet-room,
Blazing with light, and breathing with
    perfume.

There on the dais sat another king,
Wearing his robes, his crown, his signet-
    ring,
King Robert's self in features, form, and
    height,
But all transfigured with angelic light !
It was an Angel ; and his presence there
With a divine effulgence filled the air,
An exaltation, piercing the disguise,
Though none the hidden Angel recognize.

A moment speechless, motionless, amazed,
The throneless monarch on the Angel
    gazed,
Who met his look of anger and surprise
With the divine compassion of his eyes ;
Then said, " Who art thou ? and why
    com'st thou here ? "
To which King Robert answered with a
    sneer,
" I am the King, and come to claim my
    own

From an impostor, who usurps my
    throne ! ''
And suddenly, at these audacious words,
Up sprang the angry guests, and drew
    their swords ;
The Angel answered, with unruffled brow,
" Nay, not the King, but the King's
    Jester, thou
Henceforth shalt wear the bells and scal-
    loped cape,
And for thy counsellor shalt lead an ape ;
Thou shalt obey my servants when they
    call,
And wait upon my henchmen in the
    hall ! ''

Deaf to King Robert's threats and cries
    and prayers,
They thrust him from the hall and down
    the stairs ;
A group of tittering pages ran before,
And as they opened wide the folding-door,
His heart failed, for he heard, with strange
    alarms,
The boisterous laughter of the men-at-
    arms,
And all the vaulted chamber roar and ring

With the mock plaudits of " Long live the
    King ! "

Next morning, waking with the day's first
    beam,
He said within himself, " It was a
    dream ! "
But the straw rustled as he turned his
    head,
There were the cap and bells beside his
    bed,
Around him rose the bare, discolored
    walls,
Close by, the steeds were champing in
    their stalls,
And in the corner, a revolting shape,
Shivering and chattering sat the wretched
    ape.
It was no dream ; the world he loved so
    much
Had turned to dust and ashes at his
    touch !

Days came and went ; and now returned
    again
To Sicily the old Saturnian reign ;
Under the Angel's governance benign

The happy island danced with corn and
　　wine,
And deep within the mountain's burning
　　breast
Enceladus, the giant, was at rest.

Meanwhile King Robert yielded to his
　　fate,
Sullen and silent and disconsolate.
Dressed in the motley garb that Jesters
　　wear,
With look bewildered and a vacant stare,
Close shaven above the ears, as monks
　　are shorn,
By courtiers mocked, by pages laughed to
　　scorn,
His only friend the ape, his only food
What others left, — he still was unsub-
　　dued.
And when the Angel met him on his way,
And half in earnest, half in jest, would
　　say,
Sternly, though tenderly, that he might
　　feel
The velvet scabbard held a sword of steel,
" Art thou the King ? " the passion of his
　　woe

Burst from him in resistless overflow,
And, lifting high his forehead, he would
    fling
The haughty answer back, " I am, I am
    the King ! "

Almost three years were ended ; when
    there came
Ambassadors of great repute and name
From Valmond, Emperor of Allemaine,
Unto King Robert, saying that Pope Ur-
    bane
By letter summoned them forthwith to
    come
On Holy Thursday to his city of Rome.
The Angel with great joy received his
    guests,
And gave them presents of embroidered
    vests,
And velvet mantles with rich ermine
    lined,
And rings and jewels of the rarest kind.
Then he departed with them o'er the sea
Into the lovely land of Italy,
Whose loveliness was more resplendent
    made
By the mere passing of that cavalcade,

With plumes, and cloaks, and housings,
    and the stir
Of jewelled bridle and of golden spur.
And lo! among the menials, in mock
    state,
Upon a piebald steed with shambling
    gait,
His cloak of fox-tails flapping in the
    wind,
The solemn ape demurely perched behind,
King Robert rode, making huge merri-
    ment
In all the country towns through which
    they went.

The Pope received them with great pomp
    and blare
Of bannered trumpets, on Saint Peter's
    square,
Giving his benediction and embrace,
Fervent, and full of apostolic grace.
While with congratulations and with
    prayers
He entertained the Angel unawares,
Robert, the Jester, bursting through the
    crowd,
Into their presence rushed, and cried
    aloud,

"I am the King! Look, and behold in
    me
Robert, your brother, King of Sicily!
This man, who wears my semblance to
    your eyes,
Is an impostor in a king's disguise.
Do you not know me? does no voice
    within
Answer my cry, and say we are akin?"
The Pope in silence, but with troubled
    mien,
Gazed at the Angel's countenance serene;
The Emperor, laughing, said, "It is
    strange sport
To keep a madman for thy Fool at
    court!"
And the poor, baffled Jester in disgrace
Was hustled back among the populace.

In solemn state the Holy Week went by,
And Easter Sunday gleamed upon the
    sky;
The presence of the Angel, with its light,
Before the sun rose, made the city bright,
And with new fervor filled the hearts of
    men,
Who felt that Christ indeed had risen
    again.

Even the Jester, on his bed of straw,
With haggard eyes the unwonted splendor
    saw,
He felt within a power unfelt before,
And, kneeling humbly on his chamber
    floor,
He heard the rushing garments of the
    Lord
Sweep through the silent air, ascending
    heavenward.

And now the visit ending, and once more
Valmond returning to the Danube's shore,
Homeward the Angel journeyed, and
    again
The land was made resplendent with his
    train,
Flashing along the towns of Italy
Unto Salerno, and from thence by sea.
And when once more within Palermo's
    wall,
And, seated on the throne in his great
    hall,
He heard the Angelus from convent
    towers,
As if the better world conversed with
    ours,

He beckoned to King Robert to draw
    nigher,
And with a gesture bade the rest retire;
And when they were alone, the Angel
    said,
"Art thou the King?" Then, bowing
    down his head,
King Robert crossed both hands upon his
    breast,
And meekly answered him : " Thou know-
    est best !
My sins as scarlet are; let me go hence,
And in some cloister's school of peni-
    tence,
Across those stones, that pave the way to
    heaven,
Walk barefoot, till my guilty soul be
    shriven !"

The Angel smiled, and from his radiant
    face
A holy light illumined all the place,
And through the open window, loud and
    clear,
They heard the monks chant in the
    chapel near,
Above the stir and tumult of the street :

" He has put down the mighty from their
 seat,
And has exalted them of low degree ! "
And through the chant a second melody
Rose like the throbbing of a single
 string :
" I am an Angel, and thou art the King ! "

King Robert, who was standing near the
 throne,
Lifted his eyes, and lo ! he was alone !
But all apparelled as in days of old,
With ermined mantle and with cloth of
 gold ;
And when his courtiers came, they found
 him there
Kneeling upon the floor, absorbed in
 silent prayer.

THE CUMBERLAND.

T anchor in Hampton Roads we
    lay,
    On board of the Cumberland,
      sloop-of-war;
And at times from the fortress across the
    bay
    The alarum of drums swept past,
    Or a bugle blast
From the camp on the shore.

Then far away to the south uprose
    A little feather of snow-white smoke,
And we knew that the iron ship of our
    foes
    Was steadily steering its course
    To try the force
Of our ribs of oak.

Down upon us heavily runs,
    Silent and sullen, the floating fort;
Then comes a puff of smoke from her
    guns,
    And leaps the terrible death,
    With fiery breath,
From each open port.

We are not idle, but send her straight
  Defiance back in a full broadside !
As hail rebounds from a roof of slate,
    Rebounds our heavier hail
    From each iron scale
  Of the monster's hide.

" Strike your flag ! " the rebel cries,
  In his arrogant old plantation strain.
" Never ! " our gallant Morris replies ;
    " It is better to sink than to yield ! "
    And the whole air pealed
  With the cheers of our men.

Then, like a kraken huge and black,
  She crushed our ribs in her iron grasp !
Down went the Cumberland all a wrack,
    With a sudden shudder of death,
    And the cannon's breath
  For her dying gasp.

Next morn, as the sun rose over the bay,
  Still floated our flag at the mainmast
    head.
Lord, how beautiful was Thy day !
    Every waft of the air
    Was a whisper of prayer,
  Or a dirge for the dead.

Ho ! brave hearts that went down in the
    seas !
  Ye are at peace in the troubled stream ;
Ho ! brave land ! with hearts like these,
    Thy flag, that is rent in twain,
    Shall be one again,
And without a seam !

A DAY OF SUNSHINE.

 GIFT of God ! O perfect day :
Whereon shall no man work, but
    play ;
Whereon it is enough for me,
Not to be doing, but to be !

Through every fibre of my brain,
Through every nerve, through every vein,
I feel the electric thrill, the touch
Of life, that seems almost too much.

I hear the wind among the trees
Playing celestial symphonies ;
I see the branches downward bent,
Like keys of some great instrument.

And over me unrolls on high
The splendid scenery of the sky,
Where through a sapphire sea the sun
Sails like a golden galleon,

Towards yonder cloud-land in the West,
Towards yonder Islands of the Blest,
Whose steep sierra far uplifts
Its craggy summits white with drifts.

Blow, winds! and waft through all the
        rooms
The snow-flakes of the cherry-blooms!
Blow, winds! and bend within my reach
The fiery blossoms of the peach!

O Life and Love!   O happy throng
Of thoughts, whose only speech is song!
O heart of man! canst thou not be
Blithe as the air is, and as free?

WEARINESS.

LITTLE feet! that such long years
   Must wander on through hopes and fears,
     Must ache and bleed beneath your load ;
I, nearer to the wayside inn
Where toil shall cease and rest begin,
     Am weary, thinking of your road !

O little hands ! that, weak or strong,
Have still to serve or rule so long,
     Have still so long to give or ask ;
I, who so much with book and pen
Have toiled among my fellow-men,
     Am weary, thinking of your task.

O little hearts ! that throb and beat
With such impatient, feverish heat,
     Such limitless and strong desires ;
Mine, that so long has glowed and burned,
With passions into ashes turned,
     Now covers and conceals its fires.

O little souls ! as pure and white
And crystalline as rays of light

Direct from heaven, their source divine ;
Refracted through the mist of years,
How red my setting sun appears,
How lurid looks this soul of mine !

VOX POPULI.

HEN Mazárvan the Magician
  Journeyed westward through
   Cathay,
Nothing heard he but the praises
 Of Badoura on his way.

But the lessening rumor ended
 When he came to Khaledan,
There the folk were talking only
 Of Prince Camaralzaman.

So it happens with the poets :
 Every province hath its own ;
Camaralzaman is famous
 Where Badoura is unknown.

THE LEGEND BEAUTIFUL.

" HADST thou stayed, I must have
fled ! "
That is what the Vision said.

In his chamber all alone,
Kneeling on the floor of stone,
Prayed the Monk in deep contrition
For his sins of indecision,
Prayed for greater self-denial
In temptation and in trial ;
It was noonday by the dial,
And the Monk was all alone.

Suddenly, as if it lightened,
An unwonted splendor brightened
All within him and without him
In that narrow cell of stone ;
And he saw the Blessed Vision
Of our Lord, with light Elysian
Like a vesture wrapped about Him,
Like a garment round Him thrown.

Not as crucified and slain,
Not in agonies of pain,

Not with bleeding hands and feet,
Did the Monk his Master see ;
But as in the village street,
In the house or harvest-field,
Halt and lame and blind He healed,
When He walked in Galilee.

In an attitude imploring,
Hands upon his bosom crossed,
Wondering, worshipping, adoring,
Knelt the Monk in rapture lost.
Lord, he thought, in heaven that reignest,
Who am I, that thus thou deignest
To reveal thyself to me ?
Who am I, that from the centre
Of thy glory thou shouldst enter
This poor cell, my guest to be ?

Then amid his exaltation,
Loud the convent bell appalling,
From its belfry calling, calling,
Rang through court and corridor
With persistent iteration
He had never heard before.
It was now the appointed hour
When alike in shine or shower,
Winter's cold or summer's heat,

To the convent portals came
All the blind and halt and lame,
All the beggars of the street,
For their daily dole of food
Dealt them by the brotherhood ;
And their almoner was he
Who upon his bended knee,
Rapt in silent ecstasy
Of divinest self-surrender,
Saw the Vision and the Splendor.
Deep distress and hesitation
Mingled with his adoration ;
Should he go or should he stay?
Should he leave the poor to wait
Hungry at the convent gate,
Till the Vision passed away?
Should he slight his radiant guest,
Slight this visitant celestial,
For a crowd of ragged, bestial
Beggars at the convent gate ?
Would the Vision there remain ?
Would the Vision come again ?
Then a voice within his breast
Whispered, audible and clear
As if to the outward ear :
" Do thy duty ; that is best ;
Leave unto thy Lord the rest ! "

Straightway to his feet he started,
And with longing look intent
On the Blessed Vision bent,
Slowly from his cell departed,
Slowly on his errand went.

At the gate the poor were waiting,
Looking through the iron grating,
With that terror in the eye
That is only seen in those
Who amid their wants and woes
Hear the sound of doors that close,
And of feet that pass them by;
Grown familiar with disfavor,
Grown familiar with the savor
Of the bread by which men die!
But to-day, they knew not why,
Like the gate of Paradise
Seemed the convent gate to rise,
Like a sacrament divine
Seemed to them the bread and wine.
In his heart the Monk was praying,
Thinking of the homeless poor,
What they suffer and endure;
What we see not, what we see;
And the inward voice was saying:
" Whatsoever thing thou doest

To the least of mine and lowest,
That thou doest unto me ! "

Unto me ! but had the Vision
Come to him in beggar's clothing,
Come a mendicant imploring,
Would he then have knelt adoring,
Or have listened with derision,
And have turned away with loathing ?

Thus his conscience put the question,
Full of troublesome suggestion,
As at length, with hurried pace,
Towards his cell he turned his face,
And beheld the convent bright
With a supernatural light,
Like a luminous cloud expanding
Over floor and wall and ceiling.

But he paused with awe-struck feeling
At the threshold of his door,
For the Vision still was standing
As he left it there before,
When the convent bell appalling,
From its belfry calling, calling,
Summoned him to feed the poor.
Through the long hour intervening

It had waited his return,
And he felt his bosom burn,
Comprehending all the meaning,
When the Blessed Vision said,
" Hadst thou stayed, I must have fled ! "

CHARLES SUMNER.

ARLANDS upon his grave
 And flowers upon his hearse,
 And to the tender heart and
  brave
The tribute of this verse.

His was the troubled life,
 The conflict and the pain,
The grief, the bitterness of strife,
 The honor without stain.

Like Winkelried, he took
 Into his manly breast
The sheaf of hostile spears, and broke
 A path for the oppressed.

Then from the fatal field
 Upon a nation's heart

Borne like a warrior on his shield ! —
So should the brave depart.

Death takes us by surprise,
And stays our hurrying feet;
The great design unfinished lies,
Our lives are incomplete.

But in the dark unknown
Perfect their circles seem,
Even as a bridge's arch of stone
Is rounded in the stream.

Alike are life and death,
When life in death survives,
And the uninterrupted breath
Inspires a thousand lives.

Were a star quenched on high,
For ages would its light,
Still travelling downward from the sky,
Shine on our mortal sight.

So when a great man dies,
For years beyond our ken,
The light he leaves behind him lies
Upon the paths of men.

CADENABBIA.

LAKE OF COMO.

NO sound of wheels or hoof-beat
    breaks
    The silence of the summer day,
As by the loveliest of all lakes
  I while the idle hours away.

I pace the leafy colonnade,
  Where level branches of the plane
Above me weave a roof of shade
  Impervious to the sun and rain.

At times a sudden rush of air
  Flutters the lazy leaves o'erhead,
And gleams of sunshine toss and flare
  Like torches down the path I tread.

By Somariva's garden gate
  I make the marble stairs my seat,
And hear the water, as I wait,
  Lapping the steps beneath my feet.

The undulation sinks and swells
  Along the stony parapets,

And far away the floating bells
　　Tinkle upon the fisher's nets.

Silent and slow, by tower and town
　　The freighted barges come and go,
Their pendent shadows gliding down
　　By town and tower submerged below.

The hills sweep upward from the shore,
　　With villas scattered one by one
Upon their wooded spurs, and lower
　　Bellaggio blazing in the sun.

And dimly seen, a tangled mass
　　Of walls and woods, of light and shade,
Stands, beckoning up the Stelvio Pass,
　　Varenna with its white cascade.

I ask myself, Is this a dream?
　　Will it all vanish into air?
Is there a land of such supreme
　　And perfect beauty anywhere?

Sweet vision! Do not fade away:
　　Linger, until my heart shall take
Into itself the summer day,
　　And all the beauty of the lake;

Linger, until upon my brain
  Is stamped an image of the scene ;
Then fade into the air again,
  And be as if thou hadst not been.

AMALFI.

WEET the memory is to me
   Of a land beyond the sea,
   Where the waves and mountains
      meet,
Where, amid her mulberry-trees
Sits Amalfi in the heat,
Bathing ever her white feet
In the tideless summer seas.

In the middle of the town,
From its fountains in the hills,
Tumbling through the narrow gorge,
The Canneto rushes down,
Turns the great wheels of the mills,
Lifts the hammers of the forge.

'T is a stairway, not a street,
That ascends the deep ravine,

Where the torrent leaps between
Rocky walls that almost meet.
Toiling up from stair to stair,
Peasant girls their burdens bear ;
Sunburnt daughters of the soil,
Stately figures tall and straight,
What inexorable fate
Dooms them to this life of toil ?

Lord of vineyards and of lands,
Far above the convent stands.
On its terraced walk aloof
Leans a monk with folded hands ;
Placid, satisfied, serene,
Looking down upon the scene
Over wall and red-tiled roof ;
Wondering unto what good end
All this toil and traffic tend,
And why all men cannot be
Free from care and free from pain,
And the sordid love of gain,
And as indolent as he.

Where are now the freighted barks
From the marts of east and west ?
Where the knights in iron sarks
Journeying to the Holy Land,

Glove of steel upon the hand,
Cross of crimson on the breast?
Where the pomp of camp and court?
Where the pilgrims with their prayers?
Where the merchants with their wares,
And their gallant brigantines
Sailing safely into port
Chased by corsair Algerines?

Vanished like a fleet of cloud,
Like a passing trumpet-blast,
Are those splendors of the past,
And the commerce and the crowd!
Fathoms deep beneath the seas
Lie the ancient wharves and quays,
Swallowed by the engulfing waves;
Silent streets and vacant halls,
Ruined roofs and towers and walls;
Hidden from all mortal eyes
Deep the sunken city lies:
Even cities have their graves!

This is an enchanted land!
Round the headlands far away
Sweeps the blue Salernian bay
With its sickle of white sand:
Further still and furthermost

On the dim discovered coast
Pæstum with its ruins lies,
And its roses all in bloom
Seem to tinge the fatal skies
Of that lonely land of **doom.**

On his terrace, high in air,
Nothing doth the good monk care
For such worldly themes as these.
From the garden just below
Little puffs of perfume blow,
And a sound is in his ears
Of the murmur of the bees
In the shining chestnut trees ;
Nothing else he heeds or hears.
All the landscape seems to **swoon**
In the happy afternoon ;
Slowly o'er his senses creep
The encroaching waves of sleep,
And he sinks as sank the town,
Unresisting, fathoms down,
Into caverns cool and deep !

Walled about with drifts of snow,
Hearing the fierce north-wind blow,
Seeing all the landscape white,
And the river cased in ice,

Comes this memory of delight,
Comes this vision unto me
Of a long-lost Paradise
In the land beyond the sea.

BELISARIUS.

 AM poor and old and blind ;
The sun burns me, and the wind
    Blows through the city gate,
And covers me with dust
From the wheels of the august
    Justinian the Great.

It was for him I chased
The Persians o'er wild and waste,
    As General of the East ;
Night after night I lay
In their camps of yesterday ;
    Their forage was my feast.

For him, with sails of red,
And torches at mast-head,
    Piloting the great fleet,
I swept the Afric coasts

And scattered the Vandal hosts,
　　Like dust in a windy street.

For him I won again
The Ausonian realm and reign,
　　Rome and Parthenope ;
And all the land was mine
From the summits of Apennine
　　To the shores of either sea.

For him, in my feeble age,
I dared the battle's rage,
　　To save Byzantium's state,
When the tents of Zabergan
Like snow-drifts overran
　　The road to the Golden Gate.

And for this, for this, behold !
Infirm and blind and old,
　　With gray, uncovered head,
Beneath the very arch
Of my triumphal march,
　　I stand and beg my bread !

Methinks I still can hear,
Sounding distinct and near,
　　The Vandal monarch's cry,

As, captive and disgraced,
With majestic step he paced, —
 " All, all is Vanity ! "

Ah ! vainest of all things
Is the gratitude of kings ;
 The plaudits of the crowd
Are but the clatter of feet
At midnight in the street,
 Hollow and restless and loud.

But the bitterest disgrace
Is to see forever the face
 Of the Monk of Ephesus !
The unconquerable will
This, too, can bear ; — I still
 Am Belisarius !

THE HERONS OF ELMWOOD.

ARM and still is the summer
  night,
 As here by the river's brink I
  wander ;
White overhead are the stars, and white
 The glimmering lamps on the hillside
  yonder.

Silent are all the sounds of day ;
  Nothing I hear but the chirp of crick-
      ets,
And the cry of the herons winging their
      way
  O'er the poet's house in the Elmwood
      thickets.

Call to him, herons, as slowly you pass
  To your roosts in the haunts of the
      exiled thrushes,
Sing him the song of the green morass,
  And the tides that water the reeds and
      rushes.

Sing him the mystical Song of the Hern,
  And the secret that baffles our utmost
      seeking ;
For only a sound of lament we discern,
  And cannot interpret the words you are
      speaking.

Sing of the air, and the wild delight
  Of wings that uplift and winds that up-
      hold you,
The joy of freedom, the rapture of flight
  Through the drift of the floating mists
      that infold you ;

Of the landscape lying so far below,
　With its towns and rivers and desert
　　places;
And the splendor of light above, and the
　glow
Of the limitless, blue, ethereal spaces.

Ask him if songs of the Troubadours,
　Or of Minnesingers in old black-letter,
Sound in his ears more sweet than yours,
　And if yours are not sweeter and wilder
　　and better.

Sing to him, say to him, here at his gate,
　Where the boughs of the stately elms
　　are meeting,
Some one hath lingered to meditate,
　And send him unseen this friendly
　　greeting:

That many another hath done the same,
　Though not by a sound was the silence
　　broken;
The surest pledge of a deathless name
　Is the silent homage of thoughts un-
　　spoken.

A DUTCH PICTURE.

SIMON DANZ has come home
    again,
    From cruising about with his
    buccaneers ;
He has singed the beard of the King of
    Spain,
And carried away the Dean of Jaen
    And sold him in Algiers.

In his house by the Maese, with its roof
    of tiles,
    And weathercocks flying aloft in air,
There are silver tankards of antique styles,
Plunder of convent and castle, and piles
    Of carpets rich and rare.

In his tulip-garden there by the town,
    Overlooking the sluggish stream,
With his Moorish cap and dressing-gown,
The old sea-captain, hale and brown,
    Walks in a waking dream.

A smile in his gray mustachio lurks
    Whenever he thinks of the King of
    Spain,

And the listed tulips look like Turks,
And the silent gardener as he works
  Is changed to the Dean of Jaen.

The windmills on the outermost
  Verge of the landscape in the haze,
To him are towers on the Spanish coast,
With whiskered sentinels at their post,
  Though this is the river Maese.

But when the winter rains begin,
  He sits and smokes by the blazing
    brands,
And old seafaring men come in,
Goat-bearded, gray, and with double chin,
  And rings upon their hands.

They sit there in the shadow and shine
  Of the flickering fire of the winter
    night ;
Figures in color and design
Like those by Rembrandt of the Rhine,
  Half darkness and half light.

And they talk of ventures lost or won,
  And their talk is ever and ever the
    same,

While they drink the red wine of Tarragon,
From the cellars of some Spanish Don,
    Or convent set on flame.

Restless at times with heavy strides
    He paces his parlor to and fro ;
He is like a ship that at anchor rides,
And swings with the rising and falling
        tides,
    And tugs at her anchor-tow.

Voices mysterious far and near,
    Sound of the wind and sound of the sea,
Are calling and whispering in his ear,
" Simon Danz !   Why stayest thou here ?
    Come forth and follow me ! "

So he thinks he shall take to the sea
        again
    For one more cruise with his bucca-
        neers,
To singe the beard of the King of Spain,
And capture another Dean of Jaen
    And sell him in Algiers.

VITTORIA COLONNA.

NCE more, once more, Inarimé,
  I see thy purple hills! — once
    more
I hear the billows of the bay
  Wash the white pebbles on thy shore.

High o'er the sea-surge and the sands,
  Like a great galleon wrecked and cast
Ashore by storms, thy castle stands,
  A mouldering landmark of the Past.

Upon its terrace-walk I see
  A phantom gliding to and fro;
It is Colonna, — it is she
  Who lived and loved so long ago; —

Pescara's beautiful young wife,
  The type of perfect womanhood,
Whose life was love, the life of life,
  That time and change and death with-
    stood; —

For death, that breaks the marriage band
  In others, only closer pressed

The wedding-ring upon her hand
  And closer locked and barred her
    breast.

She knew the life-long martyrdom,
  The weariness, the endless pain
Of waiting for some one to come
  Who nevermore would come again.

The shadows of the chestnut trees,
  The odor of the orange blooms,
The song of birds, and, more than these,
  The silence of deserted rooms ;

The respiration of the sea,
  The soft caresses of the air,
All things in nature seemed to be
  But ministers of her despair ;

Till the o'erburdened heart, so long
  Imprisoned in itself, found vent
And voice in one impassioned song
  Of inconsolable lament.

Then as the sun, though hidden from
      sight,
  Transmutes to gold the leaden mist,

Her life was interfused with light
From realms that, though unseen, exist.

Inarimé ! Inarimé !
Thy castle on the crags above
In dust shall crumble and decay,
But not the memory of her love.

THE THREE KINGS.

HREE Kings came riding from
far away,
Melchior and Gaspar and Baltasar ;
Three Wise Men out of the East were they,
And they travelled by night and they slept
by day,
For their guide was a beautiful, wonderful star.

The star was so beautiful, large, and clear,
That all the other stars of the sky
Became a white mist in the atmosphere ;
And by this they knew that the coming
was near
Of the Prince foretold in the prophecy.

Three caskets they bore on their saddle-
    bows,
  Three caskets of gold with golden keys;
Their robes were of crimson silk with
    rows
Of bells and pomegranates and furbelows,
  Their turbans like blossoming almond-
    trees.

And so the Three Kings rode into the
    West,
  Through the dusk of night, over hill
    and dell,
And sometimes they nodded with beard
    on breast,
And sometimes talked, as they paused to
    rest,
  With the people they met at some way-
    side well.

" Of the child that is born," said Baltasar,
  " Good people, I pray you, tell us the
    news ;
For we in the East have seen his star,
And have ridden fast, and have ridden far,
  To find and worship the King of the
    Jews."

And the people answered, "You ask in
    vain ;
  We know of no king but Herod the
    Great ! "
They thought the Wise Men were men
    insane,
As they spurred their horses across the
    plain,
  Like riders in haste, and who cannot
    wait.

And when they came to Jerusalem,
  Herod the Great, who had heard this
    thing,
Sent for the Wise Men and questioned
    them ;
And said, "Go down unto Bethlehem,
  And bring me tidings of this new king."

So they rode away; and the star stood
    still,
  The only one in the gray of morn ;
Yes, it stopped, — it stood still of its own
    free will,
Right over Bethlehem on the hill,
  The city of David, where Christ was
    born.

And the Three Kings rode through the
    gate and the guard,
    Through the silent street, till their horses
        turned
And neighed as they entered the great inn-
        yard;
But the windows were closed, and the doors
    were barred,
    And only a light in the stable burned.

And cradled there in the scented hay,
    In the air made sweet by the breath of
        kine,
The little child in the manger lay,
The child, that would be king one day
    Of a kingdom not human but divine.

His mother Mary of Nazareth
    Sat watching beside his place of rest,
Watching the even flow of his breath,
For the joy of life and the terror of death
    Were mingled together in her breast.

They laid their offerings at his feet:
    The gold was their tribute to a King,
The frankincense, with its odor sweet,
Was for the Priest, the Paraclete,
    The myrrh for the body's burying.

And the mother wondered and bowed her
    head,
    And sat as still as a statue of stone ;
Her heart was troubled yet comforted,
Remembering what the Angel had said
    Of an endless reign and of David's
    throne.

Then the Kings rode out of the city gate,
    With a clatter of hoofs in proud array ;
But they went not back to Herod the
    Great,
For they knew his malice and feared his
    hate,
    And returned to their homes by another
    way.

SONG.

STAY, stay at home, my heart, and
    rest ;
    Home - keeping hearts are hap-
    piest,
For those that wander they know not
    where

Are full of trouble and full of care ;
   To stay at home is best.

Weary and homesick and distressed,
They wander east, they wander west,
And are baffled and beaten and blown
     about
By the winds of the wilderness of doubt ;
   To stay at home is best.

Then stay at home, my heart, and rest ;
The bird is safest in its nest ;
O'er all that flutter their wings and fly
A hawk is hovering in the sky ;
   To stay at home is best.

SONG FROM THE PORTUGUESE.

IF thou art sleeping, maiden,
   Awake, and open thy door ;
  'T is the break of day, and we
     must away,
O'er meadow, and mount, and moor.

Wait not to find thy slippers,
  But come with thy naked feet :

We shall have to pass through the dewy
    grass,
And waters wide and fleet.

PALINGENESIS.

 LAY upon the headland-height,
    and listened
To the incessant sobbing of the
    sea
    In caverns under me,
And watched the waves, that tossed and
    fled and glistened,
Until the rolling meadows of amethyst
    Melted away in mist.

Then suddenly, as one from sleep, I
    started ;
For round about me all the sunny capes
    Seemed peopled with the shapes
Of those whom I had known in days de-
    parted,
Apparelled in the loveliness which gleams
    On faces seen in dreams.

A moment only, and the light and glory
Faded away, and the disconsolate shore
    Stood lonely as before ;
And the wild-roses of the promontory
Around me shuddered in the wind, and
    shed
    Their petals of pale red.

There was an old belief that in the em-
    bers
Of all things their primordial form exists,
    And cunning alchemists
Could re-create the rose with all its mem-
    bers
From its own ashes, but without the bloom,
    Without the lost perfume.

Ah me ! what wonder - working, occult
    science
Can from the ashes in our hearts once
    more
    The rose of youth restore ?
What craft of alchemy can bid defiance
To time and change, and for a single hour
    Renew this phantom-flower ?

" Oh, give me back," I cried, " the van-
    ished splendors,

The breath of morn, and the exultant
    strife,
    When the swift stream of life
Bounds o'er its rocky channel, and sur-
    renders
The pond, with all its lilies, for the leap
    Into the unknown deep!"

And the sea answered, with a lamentation,
Like some old prophet wailing, and it
    said,
    "Alas! thy youth is dead!
It breathes no more, its heart has no pul-
    sation;
In the dark places with the dead of old
    It lies forever cold!"

Then said I, "From its consecrated cere-
    ments
I will not drag this sacred dust again,
    Only to give me pain;
But, still remembering all the lost endear-
    ments,
Go on my way, like one who looks before,
    And turns to weep no more."

Into what land of harvests, what planta-
    tions

Bright with autumnal foliage and the glow
    Of sunsets burning low ;
Beneath what midnight skies, whose con-
     stellations
Light up the spacious avenues between
    This world and the unseen !

Amid what friendly greetings and caresses,
What households, though not alien, yet
    not mine,
    What bowers of rest divine ;
To what temptations in lone wildernesses,
What famine of the heart, what pain and
    loss,
    The bearing of what cross !

I do not know ; nor will I vainly question
Those pages of the mystic book which
    hold
    The story still untold,
But without rash conjecture or suggestion
Turn its last leaves in reverence and good
    heed,
    Until " The End " I read.

HAWTHORNE.

MAY 23, 1864.

HOW beautiful it was, that one
          bright day
      In the long week of rain !
Though all its splendor could not chase
          away
      The omnipresent pain.

The lovely town was white with apple-
          blooms,
      And the great elms o'erhead
Dark shadows wove on their aerial looms
      Shot through with golden thread.

Across the meadows, by the gray old
          manse,
      The historic river flowed :
I was as one who wanders in a trance,
      Unconscious of his road.

The faces of familiar friends seemed
          strange ;
      Their voices I could hear,

And yet the words they uttered seemed
        to change
    Their meaning to my ear.

For the one face I looked for was not
        there,
    The one low voice was mute ;
Only an unseen presence filled the air,
    And baffled my pursuit.

Now I look back, and meadow, manse,
        and stream
    Dimly my thought defines ;
I only see — a dream within a dream —
    The hill-top hearsed with pines.

I only hear above his place of rest
    Their tender undertone,
The infinite longings of a troubled breast,
    The voice so like his own.

There in seclusion and remote from men
    The wizard hand lies cold,
Which at its topmost speed let fall the
        pen,
    And left the tale half told.

Ah! who shall lift that wand of magic
 power,
And the lost clew regain ?
The unfinished window in Aladdin's tower
 Unfinished must remain !

THE WIND OVER THE CHIMNEY.

SEE, the fire is sinking low,
 Dusky red the embers glow,
  While above them still I cower,
While a moment more I linger,
Though the clock, with lifted finger,
 Points beyond the midnight hour.

Sings the blackened log a tune
Learned in some forgotten June
 From a school-boy at his play,
When they both were young together,
Heart of youth and summer weather
 Making all their holiday.

And the night-wind rising, hark!
How above there in the dark,
 In the midnight and the snow,

Ever wilder, fiercer, grander,
Like the trumpets of Iskander,
   All the noisy chimneys blow !

Every quivering tongue of flame
Seems to murmur some great name,
   Seems to say to me, " Aspire ! "
But the night-wind answers, " Hollow
Are the visions that you follow,
   Into darkness sinks your fire ! "

Then the flicker of the blaze
Gleams on volumes of old days,
   Written by masters of the art,
Loud through whose majestic pages
Rolls the melody of ages,
   Throb the harp-strings of the heart.

And again the tongues of flame
Start exulting and exclaim :
   " These are prophets, bards, and seers ;
In the horoscope of nations,
Like ascendant constellations,
   They control the coming years."

But the night-wind cries : " Despair !
Those who walk with feet of air

Leave no long-enduring marks ;
At God's forges incandescent
Mighty hammers beat incessant,
 These are but the flying sparks.

" Dust are all the hands that wrought ;
Books are sepulchres of thought ;
 The dead laurels of the dead
Rustle for a moment only,
Like the withered leaves in lonely
 Churchyards at some passing tread."

Suddenly the flame sinks down ;
Sink the rumors of renown ;
 And alone the night-wind drear
Clamors louder, wilder, vaguer, —
" 'T is the brand of Meleager
 Dying on the hearth-stone here ! "

And I answer, — " Though it be,
Why should that discomfort me?
 No endeavor is in vain ;
Its reward is in the doing,
And the rapture of pursuing
 Is the prize the vanquished gain."

THE BELLS OF LYNN.

HEARD AT NAHANT.

 CURFEW of the setting sun !
O Bells of Lynn !
O requiem of the dying day !
O Bells of Lynn !

From the dark belfries of yon cloud-
cathedral wafted,
Your sounds aerial seem to float, O Bells
of Lynn !

Borne on the evening wind across the
crimson twilight,
O'er land and sea they rise and fall, O
Bells of Lynn !

The fisherman in his boat, far out beyond
the headland,
Listens, and leisurely rows ashore, O Bells
of Lynn !

Over the shining sands the wandering
cattle homeward
Follow each other at your call, O Bells of
Lynn !

The distant lighthouse hears, and with his
    flaming signal
Answers you, passing the watchword on,
    O Bells of Lynn!

And down the darkening coast run the
    tumultuous surges,
And clap their hands, and shout to you, O
    Bells of Lynn!

Till from the shuddering sea, with your
    wild incantations,
Ye summon up the spectral moon, O Bells
    of Lynn!

And startled at the sight, like the weird
    woman of Endor,
Ye cry aloud, and then are still, O Bells of
    Lynn!

THE HANGING OF THE CRANE.

I.

THE lights are out, and gone are
    all the guests
  That thronging came with merri-
    ment and jests
To celebrate the Hanging of the Crane
In the new house, — into the night are
    gone ;
But still the fire upon the hearth burns on,
    And I alone remain.

O fortunate, O happy day,
When a new household finds its place
Among the myriad homes of earth,
Like a new star just sprung to birth,
And rolled on its harmonious way
Into the boundless realms of space !

So said the guests in speech and song,
As in the chimney, burning bright,
We hung the iron crane to-night,
And merry was the feast and long.

II.

And now I sit and muse on what may be,
And in my vision see, or seem to see,
　Through floating vapors interfused with
　　　light,
Shapes indeterminate, that gleam and
　　　fade,
As shadows passing into deeper shade
　　Sink and elude the sight.

　For two alone, there in the hall,
　Is spread the table round and small ;
　Upon the polished silver shine
　The evening lamps, but, more divine,
　The light of love shines over all ;
　Of love, that says not mine and thine,
　But ours, for ours is thine and mine.

　They want no guests, to come between
　Their tender glances like a screen,
　And tell them tales of land and sea,
　And whatsoever may betide
　The great, forgotten world outside ;
　They want no guests ; they needs must
　　　be
　Each other's own best company.

III.

The picture fades ; as at a village fair
A showman's views, dissolving into air,
  Again   appear   transfigured   on   the
      screen,
So in my fancy this ; and now once more,
In part transfigured, through the open
    door
      Appears the selfsame scene.

Seated, I see the two again,
But not alone ; they entertain
A little angel unaware,
With face as round as is the moon,
A royal guest with flaxen hair,
Who, throned upon his lofty chair,
Drums on the table with his spoon,
Then drops it careless on the floor,
To grasp at things unseen before.

Are these celestial manners ? these
The ways that win, the arts that please ?
Ah yes ; consider well the guest,
And whatsoe'er he does seems best ;
He ruleth by the right divine
Of helplessness, so lately born

In purple chambers of the morn,
As sovereign over thee and thine.
He speaketh not; and yet there lies
A conversation in his eyes;
The golden silence of the Greek,
The gravest wisdom of the wise,
Not spoken in language, but in looks
More legible than printed books,
As if he could but would not speak.
And now, O monarch absolute,
Thy power is put to proof; for, lo!
Resistless, fathomless, and slow,
The nurse comes rustling like the sea,
And pushes back thy chair and thee,
And so good night to King Canute.

IV.

As one who walking in a forest sees
A lovely landscape through the parted
     trees,
  Then sees it not, for boughs that inter-
     vene;
Or as we see the moon sometimes revealed
Through drifting clouds, and then again
     concealed,
    So I behold the scene.

There are two guests at table now;
The king, deposed and older grown,
No longer occupies the throne, —
The crown is on his sister's brow;
A Princess from the Fairy Isles,
The very pattern girl of girls,
All covered and embowered in curls,
Rose-tinted from the Isle of Flowers,
And sailing with soft, silken sails
From far-off Dreamland into ours.
Above their bowls with rims of blue
Four azure eyes of deeper hue
Are looking, dreamy with delight;
Limpid as planets that emerge
Above the ocean's rounded verge,
Soft-shining through the summer night.
Steadfast they gaze, yet nothing see
Beyond the horizon of their bowls;
Nor care they for the world that rolls
With all its freight of troubled souls
Into the days that are to be.

v.

Again the tossing boughs shut out the
    scene,
Again the drifting vapors intervene,
    And the moon's pallid disk is hidden
        quite;

And now I see the table wider grown,
As round a pebble into water thrown
   Dilates a ring of light.

I see the table wider grown,
I see it garlanded with guests,
As if fair Ariadne's Crown
Out of the sky had fallen down ;
Maidens, within whose tender breasts
A thousand restless hopes and fears,
Forth reaching to the coming years,
Flutter awhile, then quiet lie,
Like timid birds that fain would fly,
But do not dare to leave their nests ; —
And youths, who in their strength elate
Challenge the van and front of fate,
Eager as champions to be
In the divine knight-errantry
Of youth, that travels sea and land
Seeking adventures, or pursues,
Through cities, and through solitudes
Frequented by the lyric Muse,
The phantom with the beckoning hand,
That still allures and still eludes.
O sweet illusions of the brain !
O sudden thrills of fire and frost !
The world is bright while ye remain,
And dark and dead when ye are lost !

VI.

The meadow-brook, that seemeth to stand
  still,
Quickens its current as it nears the mill ;
 And so the stream of Time that lingereth
In level places, and so dull appears,
Runs with a swifter current as it nears
  The gloomy mills of Death.

And now, like the magician's scroll,
That in the owner's keeping shrinks
With every wish he speaks or thinks,
Till the last wish consumes the whole,
The table dwindles, and again
I see the two alone remain.
The crown of stars is broken in parts ;
Its jewels, brighter than the day,
Have one by one been stolen away
To shine in other homes and hearts.
One is a wanderer now afar
In Ceylon or in Zanzibar,
Or sunny regions of Cathay ;
And one is in the boisterous camp
Mid clink of arms and horses' tramp,
And battle's terrible array.
I see the patient mother read,

With aching heart, of wrecks that float
Disabled on those seas remote,
Or of some great heroic deed
On battle-fields, where thousands bleed
To lift one hero into fame.
Anxious she bends her graceful head
Above these chronicles of pain,
And trembles with a secret dread
Lest there among the drowned or slain
She find the one beloved name.

VII.

After a day of cloud and wind and rain
Sometimes the setting sun breaks out
        again,
    And, touching all the darksome woods
        with light,
Smiles on the fields, until they laugh and
        sing,
Then like a ruby from the horizon's ring
    Drops down into the night.

What see I now? The night is fair,
The storm of grief, the clouds of care,
The wind, the rain, have passed away;
The lamps are lit, the fires burn bright,
The house is full of life and light;

It is the Golden Wedding day.
The guests come thronging in once more,
Quick footsteps sound along the floor,
The trooping children crowd the stair,
And in and out and everywhere
Flashes along the corridor
The sunshine of their golden hair.
On the round table in the hall
Another Ariadne's Crown
Out of the sky hath fallen down ;
More than one Monarch of the Moon
Is drumming with his silver spoon ;
The light of love shines over all.

O fortunate, O happy day !
The people sing, the people say.
The ancient bridegroom and the bride,
Smiling contented and serene
Upon the blithe, bewildering scene,
Behold, well pleased, on every side
Their forms and features multiplied,
As the reflection of a light
Between two burnished mirrors gleams,
Or lamps upon a bridge at night
Stretch on and on before the sight,
Till the long vista endless seems.

SONNETS.

MEZZO CAMMIN.

[Written 25 August, 1842.]

ALF of my life is gone, and I have
    let
  The years slip from me and
    have not fulfilled
The aspiration of my youth, to build
Some tower of song with lofty parapet.
Not indolence, nor pleasure, nor the fret
  Of restless passions that would not be
    stilled,
  But sorrow, and a care that almost
    killed,
  Kept me from what I may accomplish
    yet ;
Though, half-way up the hill, I see the
    Past
  Lying beneath me with its sounds and
    sights,—

A city in the twilight dim and vast,
With smoking roofs, soft bells, and gleam-
      ing lights, —
   And hear above me on the autumnal
      blast
   The cataract of Death far thundering
      from the heights.

THE EVENING STAR.

O ! in the painted oriel of the
         West,
      Whose panes the sunken sun
         incarnadines,
   Like a fair lady at her casement, shines
   The evening star, the star of love and
      rest !
And then anon she doth herself divest
   Of all her radiant garments, and re-
      clines
   Behind the sombre screen of yonder
      pines,
   With slumber and soft dreams of love
      oppressed.
O my beloved, my sweet Hesperus !

My morning and my evening star of
    love!
My best and gentlest lady! even thus,
As that fair planet in the sky above,
    Dost thou retire unto thy rest at night,
    And from thy darkened window fades
        the light.

THE CROSS OF SNOW.

N the long, sleepless watches of
        the night,
    A gentle face — the face of one
        long dead —
Looks at me from the wall, where round
    its head
The night-lamp casts a halo of pale
    light.
Here in this room she died; and soul more
    white
    Never through martyrdom of fire was
        led
    To its repose; nor can in books be
        read

The legend of a life more benedight.
There is a mountain in the distant West
    That, sun-defying, in its deep ravines
    Displays a cross of snow upon its side.
Such is the cross I wear upon my breast
    These eighteen years, through all the changing scenes
    And seasons, changeless since the day
    she died.

TO-MORROW.

IS late at night, and in the
    realm of sleep
    My little lambs are folded like
    the flocks ;
    From room to room I hear the wakeful
    clocks
    Challenge the passing hour, like guards
    that keep
Their solitary watch on tower and steep ;
    Far off I hear the crowing of the cocks,
    And through the opening door that time
    unlocks

Feel the fresh breathing of To-morrow
    creep.
To - morrow ! the mysterious, unknown
    guest,
Who cries to me : "Remember Barme-
    cide,
And tremble to be happy with the rest."
And I make answer : " I am satisfied ;
    I dare not ask ; I know not what is
    best ;
    God hath already said what shall be-
    tide."

THE BROKEN OAR.

O N C E upon Iceland's solitary
    strand
    A poet wandered with his book
    and pen,
Seeking some final word, some sweet
    Amen,
Wherewith to close the volume in his
    hand.
The billows rolled and plunged upon the
    sand,

The circling sea-gulls swept beyond his
    ken,
And from the parting cloud-rack now
    and then
Flashed the red sunset over sea and
    land.
Then by the billows at his feet was tossed
    A broken oar; and carved thereon he
      read:
    "Oft was I weary, when I toiled at
      thee";
And, like a man who findeth what was
    lost,
    He wrote the words, then lifted up his
      head,
    And flung his useless pen into the sea.

DIVINA COMMEDIA.

I.

FT have I seen at some cathedral
    door
    A laborer, pausing in the dust
      and heat,
Lay down his burden, and with reverent
    feet

Enter, and cross himself, and on the
    floor
Kneel to repeat his paternoster o'er ;
    Far off the noises of the world retreat ;
    The loud vociferations of the street
    Become an undistinguishable roar.
So, as I enter here from day to day,
    And leave my burden at this minster
        gate,
    Kneeling in prayer, and not ashamed to
        pray,
The tumult of the time disconsolate
    To inarticulate murmurs dies away,
    While the eternal ages watch and wait.

II.

How strange the sculptures that adorn
    these towers !
    This crowd of statues, in whose folded
        sleeves
    Birds build their nests ; while canopied
        with leaves
    Parvis and portal bloom like trellised
        bowers,
And the vast minster seems a cross of
    flowers !

But fiends and dragons on the gar-
    goyled eaves
Watch the dead Christ between the liv-
    ing thieves,
And, underneath, the traitor Judas low-
    ers!
Ah! from what agonies of heart and
    brain,
What exultations trampling on despair,
What tenderness, what tears, what hate
    of wrong,
What passionate outcry of a soul in pain,
    Uprose this poem of the earth and air,
    This mediæval miracle of song!

III.

I enter, and I see thee in the gloom
    Of the long aisles, O poet saturnine!
    And strive to make my steps keep pace
        with thine.
    The air is filled with some unknown
        perfume;
The congregation of the dead make room
    For thee to pass; the votive tapers
        shine;
    Like rooks that haunt Ravenna's groves
        of pine

The hovering echoes fly from tomb to
tomb.
From the confessionals I hear arise
Rehearsals of forgotten tragedies,
And lamentations from the crypts be-
low;
And then a voice celestial that begins
With the pathetic words, "Although
your sins
As scarlet be," and ends with " as the
snow."

IV.

With snow-white veil and garments as of
flame,
She stands before thee, who so long ago
Filled thy young heart with passion and
the woe
From which thy song and all its splendors came ;
And while with stern rebuke she speaks
thy name,
The ice about thy heart melts as the
snow
On mountain heights, and in swift overflow
Comes gushing from thy lips in sobs of
shame.

Thou makest full confession ; and a gleam,
　As of the dawn on some dark forest
　　cast,
　Seems on thy lifted forehead to in-
　　crease ;
Lethe and Eunoe — the remembered
　　dream
　And the forgotten sorrow — bring at
　　last
　That perfect pardon which is perfect
　　peace.

v.

I lift mine eyes, and all the windows blaze
　With forms of Saints and holy men who
　　died,
　Here martyred and hereafter glorified ;
　And the great Rose upon its leaves dis-
　　plays
Christ's Triumph, and the angelic rounde-
　　lays,
　With splendor upon splendor multi-
　　plied ;
　And Beatrice again at Dante's side
　No more rebukes, but smiles her words
　　of praise.

And then the organ sounds, and unseen
    choirs
  Sing the old Latin hymns of peace and
    love
  And benedictions of the Holy Ghost;
And the melodious bells among the spires
  O'er all the house-tops and through
    heaven above
  Proclaim the elevation of the Host!

VI.

O star of morning and of liberty!
  O bringer of the light, whose splendor
    shines
  Above the darkness of the Apennines,
  Forerunner of the day that is to be!
The voices of the city and the sea,
  The voices of the mountains and the
    pines,
  Repeat thy song, till the familiar lines
  Are footpaths for the thought of Italy!
Thy fame is blown abroad from all the
    heights,
  Through all the nations, and a sound is
    heard
  As of a mighty wind, and men devout,

Strangers of Rome, and the new prose-
   lytes,
   In their own language hear thy won-
      drous word,
   And many are amazed and many doubt.

✣

SEVEN SONNETS AND A CANZONE.

[FROM MICHAEL ANGELO.]

I.

THE ARTIST.

NOTHING the greatest artist can
      conceive
      That every marble block doth
         not confine
Within itself ; and only its design
The hand that follows intellect can
   achieve.
The ill I flee, the good that I believe,
   In thee, fair lady, lofty and divine,
   Thus hidden lie ; and so that death be
      mine,

Art, of desired success, doth me be-
  reave.
Love is not guilty, then, nor thy fair face,
  Nor fortune, cruelty, nor great disdain,
  Of my disgrace, nor chance nor destiny,
If in thy heart both death and love find
  place
  At the same time, and if my humble
    brain,
  Burning, can nothing draw but death
    from thee.

II.

FIRE.

Not without fire can any workman mould
  The iron to his preconceived design,
  Nor can the artist without fire refine
  And purify from all its dross the gold ;
Nor can revive the phœnix, we are told,
  Except by fire.   Hence if such death be
    mine
  I hope to rise again with the divine,
  Whom death augments, and time cannot
    make old.

O sweet, sweet death ! O fortunate fire
    that burns
  Within me still to renovate my days,
  Though **I am** almost numbered with
    the dead !
If by its nature unto heaven returns
  This element, me, kindled in its **blaze,**
  Will it bear upward when my life is
    fled.

III.

YOUTH AND AGE.

OH give **me** back the days when **loose**
    and free
  To my blind passion were the curb and
    rein,
  Oh give me back the angelic face again,
  With which all virtue buried seems to
    be !
Oh give my panting footsteps back to me,
  That are in age so slow and fraught
    with pain,
  And fire and moisture in the heart and
    brain,

If thou wouldst have me burn and
    weep for thee !
If it be true thou livest alone, Amor,
    On the sweet-bitter tears of human
      hearts,
    In an old man thou canst not wake
      desire ;
Souls that have almost reached the other
      shore
    Of a diviner love should feel the darts,
    And be as tinder to a holier fire.

IV.

OLD AGE.

THE course of my long life hath reached
    at last,
    In fragile bark o'er a tempestuous sea,
    The common harbor, where must ren-
      dered be
Account of all the actions of the past.
The impassioned phantasy, that, vague
    and vast,
    Made art an idol and a king to me,
    Was an illusion, and but vanity

Were the desires that lured me and
   harassed.
The dreams of love, that were so **sweet**
      of yore,
   What are they now, when two **deaths**
      may be mine, —
   One sure, and one forecasting its
      alarms?
Painting and sculpture satisfy no more
   The soul now turning to the Love
      Divine,
   That oped, to embrace us, on the **cross**
      its arms.

V.

TO VITTORIA COLONNA.

LADY, how can it chance — yet this we see
   In long experience — that will longer
      last
   A living **image** carved from quarries
      vast
   Than its own maker, who dies **pres-**
      ently?
Cause yieldeth to effect if this so be,

And even Nature is by Art surpassed ;
 This know I, who to Art have given
  the past,
 But see that Time is breaking faith with
  me.
Perhaps on both of us long life can I
 Either in color or in stone bestow,
 By now portraying each in look and
  mien ;
So that a thousand years after we die,
 How fair thou wast, and I how full of
  woe,
 And wherefore I so loved thee, may be
  seen.

VI.

TO VITTORIA COLONNA.

WHEN the prime mover of my many sighs
 Heaven took through death from out
  her earthly place,
 Nature, that never made so fair a face,
 Remained ashamed, and tears were in
  all eyes.
O fate, unheeding my impassioned cries !

O hopes fallacious! O thou spirit of
　grace,
Where art thou now?　Earth holds in
　its embrace
Thy lovely limbs, thy holy thoughts the
　skies.
Vainly did cruel death attempt to stay
　The rumor of thy virtuous renown,
　That Lethe's waters could not wash
　　away!
A thousand leaves, since he hath stricken
　thee down,
　Speak of thee, nor to thee could Heaven
　　convey,
　Except through death, a refuge and a
　　crown.

VII.

DANTE.

What should be said of him cannot be
　said ;
　By too great splendor is his name at-
　　tended ;
　To blame is easier those who him
　　offended,

Than reach the faintest glory round
   him shed.
This man descended to the doomed and
   dead
  For our instruction ; then to God as-
    cended ;
  Heaven opened wide to him its portals
    splendid,
  Who from his country's, closed against
    him, fled.
Ungrateful land ! To its own prejudice
  Nurse of his fortunes ; and this showeth
    well,
  That the most perfect most of grief
    shall see.
Among a thousand proofs let one suffice,
  That as his exile hath no parallel,
  Ne'er walked the earth a greater man
    than he.

VIII.

CANZONE.

Ah me ! ah me ! when thinking of the
   years,
  The vanished years, alas, I do not find

Among them all one day that was my
　　own !
Fallacious hopes, desires of the unknown,
　Lamenting, loving, burning, and in
　　　tears,
　(For human passions all have stirred
　　　my mind,)
Have held me, now I feel and know, con-
　fined
Both from the true and good still far
　　away.
I perish day by day ;
The sunshine fails, the shadows grow
　　more dreary,
And I am near to fall, infirm and weary.

THREE FRIENDS OF MINE.

I.

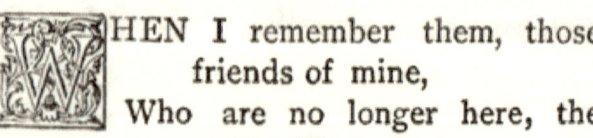HEN I remember them, those
　　　friends of mine,
　Who are no longer here, the
　　　noble three,
Who half my life were more than friends
　　to me,

And whose discourse was like a gener-
  ous wine,
I most of all remember the divine
  Something, that shone in them, and
    made us see
  The archetypal man, and what might be
  The amplitude of Nature's first design.
In vain I stretch my hands to clasp their
  hands ;
  I cannot find them. Nothing now is
    left
  But a majestic memory. They mean-
    while
Wander together in Elysian lands,
  Perchance remembering me, who am
    bereft
  Of their dear presence, and, remember-
    ing, smile.

II.

In Attica thy birthplace should have been,
  Or the Ionian Isles, or where the seas
  Encircle in their arms the Cyclades,
  So wholly Greek wast thou in thy serene
And childlike joy of life, O Philhellene !
  Around thee would have swarmed the
    Attic bees ;

Homer had been thy friend, or Socrates,
And Plato welcomed thee to his de-
mesne.
For thee old legends breathed historic
breath;
Thou sawest Poseidon in the purple
sea,
And in the sunset Jason's fleece of
gold!
Oh, what hadst thou to do with cruel
Death,
Who wast so full of life, or Death with
thee,
That thou shouldst die before thou
hadst grown old!

III.

I stand again on the familiar shore,
And hear the waves of the distracted
sea
Piteously calling and lamenting thee,
And waiting restless at thy cottage
door.
The rocks, the sea-weed on the ocean
floor,
The willows in the meadow, and the
free

Wild winds of the Atlantic welcome
   me ;
Then why shouldst thou be dead, and
   come no more?
Ah, why shouldst thou be dead, when
   common men
  Are busy with their trivial affairs,
  Having and holding?   Why, when thou
   hadst read
Nature's mysterious manuscript, and then
  Wast ready to reveal the truth it bears,
  Why art thou silent?   Why shouldst
   thou be dead?

IV.

River, that stealest with such silent pace
  Around the City of the Dead, where
   lies
  A friend who bore thy name, and whom
   these eyes
  Shall see no more in his accustomed
   place,
Linger and fold him in thy soft embrace,
  And say good night, for now the west-
   ern skies
  Are red with sunset, and gray mists
   arise

Like damps that gather on a dead
    man's face.
Good night! good night! as we so oft
    have said
Beneath this roof at midnight, in the
    days
That are no more, and shall no more
    return.
Thou hast but taken thy lamp and gone
    to bed ;
I stay a little longer, as one stays
To cover up the embers that still burn.

v.

The doors are all wide open; at the gate
    The blossomed lilacs counterfeit a
        blaze,
    And seem to warm the air ; a dreamy
        haze
    Hangs o'er the Brighton meadows like
        a fate,
And on their margin, with sea-tides elate,
    The flooded Charles, as in the happier
        days,
    Writes the last letter of his name, and
        stays
    His restless steps, as if compelled to
        wait.

I also wait ; but they will come no more,
  Those friends of mine, whose presence
      satisfied
  The thirst and hunger of my heart.
      Ah me !
They have forgotten the pathway to my
      door !
  Something is gone from nature since
      they died,
  And summer is not summer, nor can be.

CHAUCER.

N old man in a lodge within a
      park ;
  The chamber walls depicted all
      around
  With portraitures of huntsman, hawk,
      and hound,
  And the hurt deer. He listeneth to
      the lark,
Whose song comes with the sunshine
      through the dark
  Of painted glass in leaden lattice bound ;
  He listeneth and he laugheth at the
      sound,

Then writeth in a book like any clerk.
He is the poet of the dawn, who wrote
  The Canterbury Tales, and his old age
  Made beautiful with song ; and as I read
I hear the crowing cock, I hear the note
  Of lark and linnet, and from every page
  Rise odors of ploughed field or flowery
    mead.

SHAKESPEARE.

 VISION as of crowded city streets,
      With human life in endless over-
        flow ;
  Thunder of thoroughfares ; trumpets
    that blow
  To battle ; clamor, in obscure retreats,
Of sailors landed from their anchored
      fleets ;
  Tolling of bells in turrets, and below
  Voices of children, and bright flowers
    that throw
  O'er garden-walls their intermingled
    sweets !
This vision comes to me when I unfold
  The volume of the Poet paramount,

Whom all the Muses loved, not one
    alone ; —
Into his hands they put the lyre of gold,
    And, crowned with sacred laurel at
        their fount,
    Placed him as Musagetes on their
        throne.

MILTON.

PACE the sounding sea-beach
    and behold
    How the voluminous billows roll
    and run,
Upheaving and subsiding, while the sun
Shines through their sheeted emerald
    far unrolled,
And the ninth wave, slow gathering fold
    by fold
    All its loose-flowing garments into one,
    Plunges upon the shore, and floods the
        dun
    Pale reach of sands, and changes them
        to gold.
So in majestic cadence rise and fall
    The mighty undulations of thy song,
    O sightless bard, England's Mæonides !

And ever and anon, high over all
Uplifted, a ninth wave, superb and
strong,
Floods all the soul with its melodious
seas.

KEATS.

HE young Endymion sleeps En-
dymion's sleep ;
The shepherd-boy whose tale
was left half told !
The solemn grove uplifts its shield of
gold
To the red rising moon, and loud and
deep
The nightingale is singing from the steep ;
It is midsummer, but the air is cold ;
Can it be death ? Alas, beside the fold
A shepherd's pipe lies shattered near
his sheep.
Lo ! in the moonlight gleams a marble
white,
On which I read : " Here lieth one
whose name
Was writ in water." And was this the
meed

Of his sweet singing? Rather let me
    write :
  "The smoking flax before it burst to
    flame
  Was quenched by death, and broken
    the bruised reed."

THE TIDES.

SAW the long line of the vacant
    shore,
    The sea-weed and the shells
      upon the sand,
  And the brown rocks left bare on every
    hand,
  As if the ebbing tide would flow no
    more.
Then heard I, more distinctly than before,
  The ocean breathe and its great breast
    expand,
  And hurrying came on the defenceless
    land
  The insurgent waters with tumultuous
    roar.
All thought and feeling and desire, I said,

Love, laughter, and the exultant joy of
    song
Have ebbed from me forever !   Sud-
    denly o'er me
They swept again from their deep ocean
    bed,
And in a tumult of delight, and strong
As youth, and beautiful as youth, up-
    bore me.

A NAMELESS GRAVE.

" A SOLDIER of the Union mus-
        tered out,"
    Is the inscription on an un-
        known grave
At Newport News, beside the salt-sea
    wave,
Nameless and dateless ; sentinel or
    scout
Shot down in skirmish, or disastrous rout
Of battle, when the loud artillery drave
Its iron wedges through the ranks of
    brave

And doomed battalions, storming the
    redoubt.
Thou unknown hero sleeping by the sea
    In thy forgotten grave ! with secret
      shame
I feel my pulses beat, my forehead burn,
When I remember thou hast given for me
    All that thou hadst, thy life, thy very
      name,
    And I can give thee nothing in return.

SLEEP.

LULL me to sleep, ye winds, whose
    fitful sound
    Seems from some faint Æolian
      harpstring caught ;
    Seal up the hundred wakeful eyes of
      thought
    As Hermes with his lyre in sleep pro-
      found
The hundred wakeful eyes of Argus bound ;
    For I am weary, and am overwrought
    With too much toil, with too much care
      distraught,

And with the iron crown of anguish
    crowned.
Lay thy soft hand upon my brow and
    cheek,
    O peaceful Sleep! until from pain re-
      leased
    I breathe again uninterrupted breath!
Ah, with what subtile meaning did the
    Greek
    Call thee the lesser mystery at the feast
    Whereof the greater mystery is death!

NATURE.

S a fond mother, when the day is
    o'er,
    Leads by the hand her little
    child to bed,
Half willing, half reluctant to be led,
And leave his broken playthings on the
    floor,
Still gazing at them through the open
    door,
    Nor wholly reassured and comforted
    By promises of others in their stead,

Which, though more splendid, may not
please him more ;
So Nature deals with us, and takes away
Our playthings one by one, and by the
hand
Leads us to rest so gently, that we go
Scarce knowing if we wish to go or stay,
Being too full of sleep to understand
How far the unknown transcends the
what we know.

THE POETS.

 YE dead Poets, who are living
still
Immortal in your verse, though
life be fled,
And ye, O living Poets, who are dead
Though ye are living, if neglect can kill,
Tell me if in the darkest hours of ill,
With drops of anguish falling fast and
red
From the sharp crown of thorns upon
your head,

Ye were not glad your errand to fulfil?
Yes; for the gift and ministry of Song
   Have something in them so divinely
      sweet,
   It can assuage the bitterness of wrong;
Not in the clamor of the crowded street,
   Not in the shouts and plaudits of the
      throng,
   But in ourselves, are triumph and defeat.

Longfellow's Poetical Works.

IN VARIOUS EDITIONS.

—◆—

Complete Poetical Works. New *Riverside Edition*, from New Electrotype plates. With Text from the last revised by the author, and including all Poems which have been authorized to appear since his death. With Notes and three Portraits. 6 vols., **crown 8vo**, the set, $9.00.

Poetical Works (including Christus). *Cambridge Edition.* With Portrait. 4 vols., 12mo, $7.00.

Poems. *Cabinet Edition.* 16mo, $1.00.
Household Edition. Portrait and Illustrations. 12mo, $1.75; full gilt, $2.00.
Family Edition. Illustrated. 8vo, $2.50.
Red-Line Edition. Illustrations and Portrait. 16mo, $2.50.
Illustrated Library Edition. Portrait and Illustrations. 8vo, $3.50.
New *Illustrated Octavo Edition.* Including the Golden Legend. With Portrait and Illustrations. 8vo, $7.50.

Christus. *Cabinet Edition.* 16mo, $1.00.
Household Edition. Illustrated. 12mo, $1.75.
Red-Line Edition. Illustrated. 16mo, $2.50.

These editions of Christus, with corresponding editions of Poems, form complete Poetical Works in two uniform volumes.

Poetical Works. *Subscription Edition.* With Portrait and over 600 Illustrations. 30 Parts, each 4to, 50 cents, *net.*

Early Poems. *Red-Line Edition.* With Portrait, etc. 12mo, $1.00, *net.*

Complete Prose Works. New *Riverside Edition*, from new plates. With Text from the last revised by the Author, Notes, Index, and Portrait. 2 vols. crown 8vo, $3.00.

Translation of the Divina Commedia of Dante. One Volume Edition. 8vo, $2.50.
Cambridge Edition. 3 vols. 12mo, $4.50.
The Same. 3 vols. royal 8vo, each $4.50.

New *Riverside Edition*, from new plates. With Text from the last revised by the Translator, with various readings, Notes, and Engraving of Bust of Longfellow. 3 vols. crown 8vo, the set, $4.50.

HOUGHTON, MIFFLIN AND COMPANY,
BOSTON AND NEW YORK.

www.ingramcontent.com/pod-product-compliance
Lightning Source LLC
Chambersburg PA
CBHW020119030726
47498CB00006B/2187